Me Among the Ruins is the fourth volume of Donald Jack's highly successful *Bandy Papers*, a series which grew out of his prize-winning first novel *Three Cheers for Me*. Subsequent volumes have continued to record the remarkable career of Bartholomew Bandy, a Canadian pilot in the First World War. Now, as the war draws to its close, Bandy's hilarious adventures take him home to Canada, where his reception as a war hero is very short-lived, and to Russia, where his talent for disruption is seen at its best in the Bolshevik revolution.

Donald Jack is an Englishman who served in the RAF himself before moving to Canada in 1951. He is well known in Canada and the United States for his plays, films and TV scripts, but *The Bandy Papers* have earned him international recognition as a humorist – *Three Cheers for Me* and *That's Me in the Middle* were both winners of the Stephen Leacock Award for Humor. Donald Jack, who lives in Toronto, is currently planning a further volume in the series.

ALSO BY DONALD JACK

Three Cheers for Me
That's Me in the Middle
It's Me Again

ME AMONG THE RUINS

The Journals of Bartholomew Bandy

Volume Four

DONALD JACK

PaperJacks

A Division of General Publishing Co. Limited
Don Mills, Ontario

Published in PaperJacks 1976

Reprinted by arrangement with Doubleday & Co. Inc.

First published with *It's Me Again*, The Bandy
Papers Vol 3, in one volume under the title *It's Me Again*

Copyright © 1976 by Donald Jack

ISBN 0 7737 7132 8

Printed in Great Britain by
Hazell Watson & Viney Ltd, Aylesbury, Bucks.

CONTENTS

Looking Shopsoiled   9

Lording It in London   18

There's Me, Among the Ruins   28

Another View of Halifax   44

Back Again   61

The Dreadful Shore   66

Disguised as a Bear   83

A Tinpot Generalissimo   101

The Train   114

Another View of the Train   127

Home   142

ME AMONG THE RUINS

Looking Shopsoiled

The reunion with Katherine was joyous, but the homecoming was kind of melancholy. As the Rolls burbled up the driveway of Burma Park, the white Georgian mansion seemed to have lost its air of serenity, as if it were aware that the Lewises were leaving it in the lurch.

It looked positively glum under the grey and sultry August sky, its curtainless windows staring hollowly at the furniture that was stacked at the edge of the great lawn, ready for the next Pickford's van.

Most of the staff were already installed in the Kensington house, except for poor old Burgess, who, like so many millions of people all over the world, was down with Spanish influenza.

Katherine's mother and father were in the echoing entrance hall, arguing about whether or not to leave their sixteenth-century sideboard behind. "I have always considered it an extremely ugly piece," Mrs. Lewis was saying, "and I don't care what good Queen Bess says. Moreover, it is ostentatiously heavy. The workmen are complaining about becoming embedded in the side garden because of its weight; and I do not wish to leave our side garden behind dotted with cloth-capped proletarians. Such socialist statuary might give the next tenants the impression that we were of an eccentric mind, or worse, that we had been reading Mr. Bernard Shaw. No, William: give me something modern in the way of furniture; for instance, Regency. You would never find a

Regency sideboard causing Pickford's to sink up to its ankles in turf."

"At the very least, we ought to take it along for firewood," Mr. Lewis said, his face lighting up at the sight of his daughter. "They say there is a great shortage of kindling at the moment, in London . . . Ah, my darling. And Bartholomew."

As he pressed my hand, he studied me keenly. "You look decidedly shopsoiled, my boy. Notoriety seems to have a wearing effect on you."

Mrs. Lewis was adorned in her travelling bonnet, the one with all the veil, that made her look as if she were swathed in ectoplasm. Her voice, however, was far from spiritualistic.

"Bartholomew," she thundered. "You are here."

"Mother!"

"There is no need to be formal, Bartholomew. You may continue to address me as Mrs. Lewis if you wish."

As I kissed her lined, haughty face, Katherine linked arms with her father and they both smiled and waited, as if settling down to enjoy a bout of amateur theatricals featuring two performers who were sufficiently well-loved for their thespian deficiencies to be overlooked.

"You seem, Bartholomew," Mrs. Lewis said severely, "to have a habit of coming home early."

"You can't get away from me that easily, Mrs. Lewis."

"Then we shall just have to put your premature arrival to good purpose. You may help move the furniture."

"Certainly, Mrs. Lewis. I have room in the car for either you or the Elizabethan sideboard."

"I hope, Bartholomew, that you are not implying that I take up as much space as the end product of a four-hundred-year-old oak tree. Incidentally, I gather you have been attracting attention to yourself again, in the public prints. Pray what vulgar display of self-advertisement have you been indulging in this time?"

"You know very well why he's in all the papers, Mama," Katherine said. "Incidentally, Bart has to go to Canada in a few days."

"Just as I feared; he *has* been disgracing himself again." She looked at me severely. "So you are being sent back to Canada, are you? Well, if you will steal, Bartholomew, you must be prepared to suffer for it."

As the kitchen had been cleaned out down to the last cockroach, and as the dining room was also stark naked, we had lunch among the roses in the west garden, using a bench dragged from the greenhouse by Katherine and her father (with me, of course, supervising the operation).

It was a delightfully frivolous picnic that even Mr. Lewis' news could not spoil. He had been in touch with the American Embassy, he said, to enquire about the Stevens Life-Pack parachute.

"Ah!"

"It's not very good, Bart. The U. S. Army evaluated the Stevens parachute some time ago, as well as the Broadwick Safety Pack, along with one or two others. They found none of them suitable for aircraft use."

"Ah."

After lunch, Mrs. Lewis went off to hound and chivvy the moving men, and Mr. Lewis went back to the library to finish packing his books, where he was found, two hours later, walled in by still uncrated tomes and reading a particularly sordid passage from Walter Pater.

Meanwhile Katherine and I went for a last stroll across the sward. The air was hot but sunless. Swallows dived and zoomed over the grass.

"Don't know how you can look so happy, leaving this place," I said dismally.

"It's not the end of the world, darling. We'll have just as much fun in London."

"Won't be the same at all."

"You gloomy old thing," Katherine said affectionately, squeezing my arm. "You'd think it was you who'd been born and brought up at Burma Park, not me."

The heat billowed around us as we tramped onward across the enormous lawn.

"I suppose all the furniture's out of your rooms upstairs as well, is it?"

— "M'm," she said, flicking a mischievous glance at me. "Including the bed."

"Huh. And we won't be settled into the other house until tomorrow night, either."

"Papa's booked us a room at the Ritz for tonight."

"That's hours away."

Katherine whistled a few bars from Stravinsky, then said off-handedly, "You said before you left you wondered how you'd be able to hold out. Did you—" She took an unsteady breath, trying to look as if it didn't matter in the least. "Did you manage?"

"It was quite a struggle."

She glowed, and took my hand as we turned onto the trail through the east woods. The air among the trees was hot and heavy, and we had to keep stepping off the path to avoid all the dogfighting gnats.

We stopped and kissed among the ferns, murmuring daft endearments.

"Oh, darling, why do you have to go away again?"

"'s only for a short time."

"I suppose you'll receive quite a hero's welcome back home."

"M'yes. They want me to help restore morale on the home front."

"If they only knew what they were letting themselves in for."

"Howjamean?"

"The idea of you restoring morale. You're more likely to cause a riot."

"I better take your mother. She'd soon quell it."

We walked on again. As the path narrowed, Katherine moved ahead. She was wearing a long grey dress, the thin material stroking and caressing her flanks as she moved. I felt myself becoming engorged with desire. My heart started sending out jungle messages.

"The *Express* says you'll probably be getting the Victoria Cross. I was pasting that bit in my scrapbook last night. They said it was perhaps the greatest *coup* of the war."

"*Coup* lummy."

"Tell me about it again," she said, as we drew abreast once more. She hugged my arm to her excitedly.

I caught sight of a mossy bank over to the left, beneath an oak tree. It was surrounded by ferns, and had a suggestive hollow in the middle, which looked perfect for a pair of hips. Two pairs, in fact.

"I've already told you twice," I said.

"What's the matter? Your face has gone all red."

"Katherine. Let's go over there."

She looked at me wide-eyed. "Here? In the open?"

"Yes. Why not?"

She began to breathe faster, and turned red as well. "Oh, Bart," she said, shivering in the heat.

"Come on. Come on."

In fact she was already hurrying through the crackling ferns. I was panting by the time I caught up with her. I squatted down to feel the moss.

"It's wonderfully springy," I husked.

"What if somebody comes?"

"We can pretend we're rooting for truffles."

She snorted breathlessly and started to remove her dress; but then: "I'm shy."

I kissed her for as long as I could hold my breath, then sank down and rose again, my hands full of hem; then spent a frantic half minute wrenching at my Sam-Browne, kicking off my shoes, and unsticking my shirt.

*　*　*　*　*　*

It was all over in about two damn minutes. As we lay panting and twitching on the moss, a bunch of gnats came over to see what all the hubbub was about, and hovered over our gleaming forms.

"That was short but sweet. Oh, darling, I do love you."

"Me, too."

"You certainly have been saving up."

"Lots left in the bank, too."

"Oh, Bart . . . I feel so lucky and so happy. I love you with all my heart."

"Did you know there was an earwig in your navel?"

A shriek, then faces contorted with laughter, slowly softening into barrierless love.

"Oh, hell, I've lost my shoe."

I'd kicked it so far into the woods it took us minutes to find it again.

"I wonder," Katherine said as we walked back, "what it would be like, doing it up a tree?"

As we strolled back across the lawn, bumping gently against each other, Katherine asked me to tell her all about it again.

* B. W. Bandy left instructions that these asterisks should be left intact, in spite of editorial pressure for the usual filthy sex scene.

"Specially the bit where you turned up at your squadron and they were so overjoyed to see you again."

So I told her about it once more, but making an effort, this time, to recount it as it really happened, rather than in the way it had been described in the newspapers.

I had related the story so often, to sundry pilots, staff officers, and war correspondents, and had subsequently read so many differing versions, that it was already getting quite hard to sort out what had actually happened. For the benefit of their readers, i.e., for dramatic purposes, the correspondents had melted down and recast the untidy shape of the action in a neater and more symmetrical mould. In particular, they had reshaped the basic fact, which was, of course, that I'd merely been making desperate efforts to save my own skin. The fact that I'd saved it in a plane that the authorities were particularly anxious to acquire was purely accidental. But at least one newspaper said I'd deliberately lured down the new Fokker with the express purpose of acquiring it for the Allies, basing this on the assumption that no pilot who had shot down twenty-two e.a. in three months could possibly be vanquished by one miserable Jerry.

Odd's blood.

"It must have caused a tremendous sensation when you came back in a German plane," Katherine said, her dark eyes alight with anticipation, though I'd already told her twice about the reception at R.A.F. H.Q., and about being congratulated by Haig's Chief of Intelligence, and getting a telegram from the King, and being photographed for the *Illustrated London News*.

"Go on, tell me what they said when you got back to your squadron."

"I honestly don't remember too well, Katherine. I'd just had a decidedly blotto session at Wing."

"No, go on. About them all cheering like mad."

"They were really applauding my luck."

"Oh, don't make me sick."

"It's true. Pilots appreciate good luck much more than feats of derring-do. Mind you, I pretended all the praise and plaudits and stuff was only my due. I was very lordly and casual about it all . . ."

The squadron hadn't been informed that I had got back safely, and the mess was so hushed as I staggered up to the house I thought they'd all gone to bed.

14

They were nearly all there, however, including Carson. He had managed to get back, after crashing on the front lines. Some Tommies, he said, had counted eighty bullet holes in his machine before giving up and going back to their game of bezique.

When I walked in, putting one drunken foot carefully in front of the other, they couldn't believe their eyes. Carson had told them about the fight, and Artillery had confirmed his account. Under the perfect weather conditions prevailing, their spotters had watched the whole show through field glasses. Three Dolphins had gone down, they reported. The fourth, after disposing of four of the enemy, had disappeared behind a hill. Two minutes later, dense black smoke had rolled into the sky.

They had all thought me burned to a crisp, or badly wounded, but in either condition, quite definitely in enemy hands.

"How could you possibly have escaped?" Derby asked; and when I told him, he laughed so much that tears poured down his cheeks.

"The men have been coming up to us all evening, asking if we'd heard any news of you," Orville said. "The colonel came too, even though it was after dark. He said we'd never see your like again."

"I bet he looked relieved."

"He managed to conceal it pretty well."

"Hell, we ought to've known you'd get back somehow," Derby snorted, "and make a profit on it, into the bargain."

"And the next day," Katherine said, "you were called to Canadian H.Q."

"Yes. And—"

"And the Canadian Minister for Overseas Forces told you you were going home on leave."

"Yes. And—"

"And they were in process of forming the Canadian Air Force, and you were to be given a wing."

"That's right. Go on, I'm dying to hear the rest."

"No, you tell it, darling. About how excited they were in Canada about your exploit, and they wanted you to make speeches at Peace Bond rallies, and the Prime Minister was anxious to meet you, and everything."

"M'm."

"Well, go on! Tell me!"

"We had great difficulty in persuading the R.A.F. to give you up," the Minister confided over lunch that day. "They must obviously have thought very highly of you, Bandy, even before that exploit of yours. You've no idea what determined and subtle efforts the British made to keep you in the R.A.F."

"Really?"

"The Air Minister was particularly crafty about it, in that sly British way of his. When I told him we wanted you transferred, he acceded to our request with alacrity."

"Natch—eh?"

"It was their devilishly clever strategy, my boy. They were attempting to lower your value in our eyes, by simulating relief and satisfaction. Hoping, you see, that we would begin to wonder if you were really worth having. You know, to make us feel insecure. They're always trying to make us feel insecure, you know.

"I must confess that I did in fact experience a faint twinge of doubt in the face of their apparently overwhelming relief at the prospect of losing you. But don't worry, I saw through their crafty strategy in time and immediately rendered it abortive by the simple process of pretending not to see through it. I reaffirmed our determination to have you, Bandy, and nothing the Air Minister could say would change my mind. So the whole matter," the Minister said triumphantly, "was concluded in a matter of minutes."

Well, at least the pilots had been flatteringly reluctant to lose me. At the farewell dinner at Montonvillers, attended by the C.O.s of about half a dozen squadrons, and honored once again by the presence of the G.O.C., Captain Derby had made one of the best drunken speeches I'd ever heard—especially as it was all about me.

"When he first arrived, we all felt certain," John said, standing at the head of the table, grave and spifflicated, "that no good could come of a C.O. who looked like a pantomime horse that had strayed by mistake into the nearest abattoir. And we were—hic-hug—right. We used to be simple, loyal, dutiful offishers, utterly honest, obedient an', an' upright. Now look at us: half of us look as if we'll never be upright again.

"There are so many stories about Major Bartholomew that one doesn't know whether one is faced with an embarrassment of riches or a richness of embarrassment. The time he and Lieutenant France, for instance, joined the men's football game, riding a couple of motor bikes, and ended up charging each other with the goalposts, like demented knights of yore—or should I say gore; or the time he jumped on a certain prize peacock; or the time he wangled several new Nissens from the Royal Engineers, after presenting them with a chit signed by none other than D Haig himself—Lance Corporal Dougal Haig, that is, one of our engine fitters . . ."

He mentioned one or two other incidents, but after he referred to me as Major Foxfurs, by the time the screeches of laughter had died down he had forgotten where he was.

"Major Bandy," he went on, turning owlishly to the G.O.C., "has had a simply shocking effect on this squadron, General, I'm sorry to tell you. Among other things, teaching us to be so considerate to the other ranks that now the blighters won't work more than twenty-one hours a day on those frightful Hispano-Suiza engines . . . but above all, encouraging us circumspect chaps to emulate his example of being so frightful in battle that I hear the Jerry Air Force is seriously thinking of adding hair dye to their standard equipment—their flying helmets, blood sausages, pipeclay, whips, monocles and the like—the dye being for the benefit of Hun pilots whose hair has turned white overnight after meeting our redoubtable C.O. . . ."

When the cheers had died down, he ended gravely, "All the same, I know there is not a single pilot who is not deeply chagrined at the thought that we are no longer to be stricken by the sight of that often dishevelled figure in fox furs and bicycle clips, surmounted by that insurmountable face that can only be described as indescribable, as he lurches about the airfield inspiring the men to devoted labor and the pilots to a martial determination that does not entirely deny the possibility that they are perhaps a little more than mere cannon-fodder. Major Bandy may be the most infuriating, tactless, undignified, deplorable, larcenous, and mulish individual on the face of this earth—but, by God, he's offensive!"

"I tried to explain what Derby meant," I said to Katherine. "He just meant I was a bit aggressive in combat; but the fellows were making so much racket I don't think they got that bit."

Lording It in London

Two hours later, we left Burma Park forever.

I was the only one to look back, as the huge Georgian house sank slowly into the Berkshire foliage. The others were too busy quarreling about who had sat on the tomatoes.

Mr. and Mrs. Lewis were staying the night with friends, and so Katherine and I put up at the Ritz. It was pretty expensive: 15s. 6d. incl. bth., but as I explained to Katherine, the Spartan Hotel, where I'd always stayed before, just wasn't good enough for me any more.

We were given a room that was said to have an excellent view of Green Park, but somehow we never got around to confirming this, as Katherine was so anxious to make up for lost time. She acted almost as if sex were quite natural, if occasionally rather comical and absurd, and was even willing to try some of the unforgettably shocking variations I'd read about in *Fanny Hill of Sunnybrook Farm*. Or was it *Rebecca?*

Finally, however, we were driven out of the bed, the armchair, and the bathtub by starvation. As we floated bonelessly into the restaurant, there was quite a stir among the guests, and a craning of necks.

For an awful moment, I thought they were gawking like that because they could divine, through some subtle dishevelment in our manner, that we had just been making love. Before dinner, too, my dear. However, I told myself firmly that this reaction was merely a tribute to my renown. To my surprise, this was confirmed a couple of minutes later when a tall schoolgirl, all teeth and elbows, came blushing up for my autograph, and the headwaiter presented us with a complimentary bottle of Bulmer's Cider.

It was pleasant enough being famous, but I'm afraid I couldn't restrain a certain cynicism during those few days that remained before I sailed for Canada. It was only about four months since I had been just as much an object of public attention; only then I had been regarded with fury and loathing.

Nobody seemed to remember that scandal now. One couldn't help reflecting that fame was sure to be just as fleeting as notoriety. In some ways, the two were hard to tell apart.

Not that I failed to take advantage of the new esteem. I swanked modestly in the approved R.A.F. manner throughout all the subsequent interviews, dinners, and other social occasions. I particularly enjoyed the deference shown me during the demonstration at Martlesham Heath, where the new Fokker was dismaying the experts with its advanced, tubular-steel construction and its exceptional maneuverability, speed, and climbing power.

There was also the visit to Drury Lane, where an adaptation of Bach's cantata *Phoebus and Pan* was being repeated, owing to lack of popular demand, and where my presence in the audience was announced from the stage just after the intermission.

This drew an enthusiastic round of applause from those members of the audience who had not already left. Following the show, Katherine and I were invited backstage to meet the conductor, Sir Thomas Beecham.

"I perform on the pianoforte myself, occasionally," I smirked.

"You perform *what* on the piano? Hand stands? Card tricks?"

"No, no, Sir Thomas. I mean I tickle the ivories on occasion."

"If you mean you play the piano, why the devil don't you say so?" Sir Thomas snapped.

I could see the conductor was in a bad mood, because of all those empty seats. Still, I couldn't let him get away with that. After all, I was a great man, with my picture in the papers and everything, while he was just another conductor, with no future to speak of, judging by *his* reviews.

"That's all right, Sir Thomas," I said. "You can snap at me all you like, old man. I mean, it's not my fault if one of your clarinets squeaked during a particularly ill-rehearsed *pianissimo* passage. But if it relieves your feelings, you go right ahead, I don't mind," I said, looking extremely indulgent.

Sir Thomas turned his basilisk stare on me for a moment before wheeling on his concert-master, who was looking quite frightened. "Who did you say he was—former music critic of the Ramsbottom *Gazette?*" Which I must admit was rather a neat way of pretending not to know who I was. Unless—no, no, he was *bound* to have heard of me, absolutely bound to.

It was just like old times, being back in the Air Ministry in the Strand. Even the general attitude to the Secretary of State was familiar: he was just as unpopular as the last one had been.

However, he greeted me, initially anyway, with such affability that for a while I thought he really had called me in merely to offer his congratulations.

"Yes, it was a very dashing exploit, there's no doubt about that," the Minister said, sketching airplanes on his desk pad with a Ministry of Works pencil.

"'m'kew."

"Nor must we overlook the work you did with the squadron, Bandy. The G.O.C. waxed most eloquent on your work in turning an exceedingly smart and dutiful squadron into the most thoroughly disreputable collection of bandits operating on the Western Front."

He uttered a brief laugh to show that he was just indulging in a little verbal playfulness.

"No, but seriously, though your methods were perhaps a trifle contumacious, there's certainly no doubt about the result. The G.O.C. informs me that in July your squadron accounted for the third-highest total of kills, after 43 and 56 squadrons."

He started to sketch a French guillotine, complete with a basket of heads. "In a separate dispatch, by the way," the Minister continued, intent on his work, "he asked that something be done about the parachute situation, pointing, among other things, to their increasing use by the enemy.

"I told him, Bandy, that it's not quite as simple as that. Our production facilities are already strained to the utmost. Now that we and the French are supplying the Americans with air equipment, we're having difficulty in keeping up even with the demands for aircraft, let alone ancillary equipment."

I cleared my throat and started to speak, but the Minister continued firmly, "However, in spite of the difficulties, and in view of the growing concern in, ah, certain quarters, I have informed him that I have given orders for the Guardian Angel to be put into production forthwith, with the intention of distributing it in quantity among the front-line squadrons later this year."

"That's very interesting news, sir," I began.

"Yes, I thought you'd be pleased, Bandy. You know," he said heartily, "you've given us a good deal of trouble over this business. Causing dissension among your superior officers, and the nervous prostration of at least one brigade commander, and instigating questions in Parliament, and so forth. And now I see you're using this temporary fame of yours to make outspoken comments on the subject to the press.

"It may be unreasonable of us, Bandy, but we don't particularly enjoy being accused of indifference to the lives of our airmen." He started to shade in the guillotine blade. He also added another head to the basket. "I must remind you, Bandy, that whatever your government's future plans for you, you're still in the Royal Air Force, and subject to our discipline. So—" He glanced up with a smile. "I'd be personally obliged if in future you would desist from giving interviews to the press on other than personal matters."

He screwed up the paper and dropped it decisively into the waste bin, and leaned back, smiling again. "Anyway, now that something is being done about it, that should be a satisfactory conclusion to the affair, don't you agree? Let me see, now, is there anything else . . . ?"

"The only trouble, sir . . ."

"What's that?"

"The Guardian Angel is almost as dangerous as the situation it's designed to alleviate."

The Minister's smile froze solid. "What?"

"Your Chief of Air Staff's assistant was good enough to let me see that fat file on the Guardian Angel, sir. With all those unfavorable reports, which I heartily endorse—" (Gad, I was getting quite good at High-Grade Civil Servantese) "—after having tried it out for myself, I don't see how you can send a parachute like that to the squadrons."

The Minister seemed able to change his racial characteristics at will. His face turned quite black. "But it's as a result of your damned interference that I've ordered it to be rushed into production!" he shouted.

"Can't help that, sir. It's no good, and it never will be. It'll put the pilots at an impossible disadvantage.

"You see, sir," I said, crossing my legs and delicately folding the crease of my trousers sideways over my knee, "while it may get a pilot out of difficulties, its constricting effect in the cockpit will in many cases contribute to those difficulties. The pilot won't be able to move the controls freely enough.

"By Jove, sir, there's irony for you, isn't it!" I exclaimed, smiling like anything and even giving a little laugh. "The very apparatus designed to get a pilot out of a crippled aircraft, is likely to be the very thing that causes the aircraft to be crippled in the first place. By Jove, what irony," I said with an appreciative twitch of the head at the sheer irony of it.

The Air Minister was now starting to keen like a darkie as well, and clench and unclench his fists in a rather impotent, speechless sort of way.

"However, Minister, don't despair," I went on soothingly. "I've just learned about another British parachute, the best design I've ever come across, called the Prentice parachute. It—"

"Get out!" the Minister shouted. "Get out!" He sounded uncannily like his friend Soames.

"No, but sir, just let me tell you about the Prentice parachute. It's been designed by a man who, by some amazing coincidence, is called Mr. Prentice. It—"

But the Minister just wouldn't listen. In fact, he was already calling for the entire corps of commissionaires to come up and manhandle me out of the building, so I had no alternative but to get up and run for it.

Really. The brass were a terribly unreasonable and illogical lot, when you got right down to it.

I'd learned about the Prentice design only the day before. Mr. Lewis' M.P. friend, Mr. Davenport, had rung up to say he was sending along a man called Prentice, who had something interesting to add to the parachute controversy. In fact, Davenport said, he was thinking of using Prentice as a fresh weapon with which to belabor the government.

Mr. Prentice arrived at the Lewis house in Kensington while I was upstairs making myself spruce and smart for another portrait sitting.*

When I came down, it took me a minute or so to find him and Mr. Lewis, among all the books stacked several feet deep in the library.

"Mr. Prentice is with the Vickers design staff," Mr. Lewis murmured.

"It's a great honor to meet you, Mr. Bandy," said the visitor, gazing at my face as if glimpsing Canterbury Cathedral or the Hammersmith Underground Lavatory for the first time.

"Course. I mean, yes, thank you."

"I won't keep you more than a few minutes," Mr. Prentice said ingratiatingly. "I can see I've interrupted you in the middle of your nap."

Eh? I looked uncertainly at my best uniform. Surely it didn't look as if I'd been sleeping in it?

"I've read all about you, of course. I've been particularly interested in your comments about parachutes."

"Mr. Prentice has been working on a new design since 1916, Bart," Mr. Lewis said.

"Oh?" I sat on a pile of encyclopedias and looked interestedly at Mr. Prentice. He was an elderly little man—well into his thirties—in a crumpled suit, and he had a peculiar habit of making tentative, clutching motions at his unspeakables, as if he'd recently caught crabs and was trying to remember not to claw at them in mixed company. And Mr. Lewis and I were certainly mixed company.

"My work is really in aeronautical dynamics," he said, his blue eyes apologetic yet determined, as if he expected to be thrown out of the house but was going to have his say beforehand. "But, as Mr. Lewis indicated, I've had some interest in parachutes for quite some time, and, well, I've done a fair amount of work on a design of my own."

* This portrait of Bandy, by Sir Alfred Munnings, who specialized in horse pictures, can, with some persistence, be seen at the National Portrait Gallery in London, where it has been carefully stored in the cellars. Ed.

23

"Manual or automatic?"

"Oh, manual, of course. Automatic types are just too risky. I've
. I've brought one along, as a matter of fact, in case you had a
moment to . . ."

"You've brought a parachute?"

Mr. Prentice struggled up and looked around anxiously. "Let me
see, where did I . . . ?"

He eventually found it behind a stack of display cases in which
Mr. Lewis kept his prize ferns. Ferns were Mr. Lewis' hobby.

I looked at the parachute in astonishment. "That's a parachute?"

"I know it's unusually small, but it's the way the silk is machine-
sewn, and the way the shroud lines are arranged, you see . . ."

I hefted it. It weighed only about twelve pounds, including the
harness. It was smaller than a hiker's rucksack and a good deal
flatter.

I was tremendously excited—until Mr. Prentice opened it. It
required only a sharp tug at a wooden ring to spill the parachute
onto the carpet.

I looked at his creation blankly for a moment, then backed away
cautiously. The man was a lunatic. The parachute was only two
feet wide.

"M'yes, very interesting," I said, wearing a carefully inscrutable
expression so as not to send him completely over the edge. "M'yes
. . . but don't you think—" I cleared my throat. "Don't you think
it's a trifle, well, small, to support the weight of a 160-pound pilot?"

Mr. Prentice smiled. "Oh, no," he said. "That's just the . . . Well,
I'll show you." And he gathered up the parachute and started to
back away. As the shroud lines of the teeny parachute tautened,
other material appeared, and swirled over and around the stacks
of books that littered the library floor. He stopped after several
square yards of white silk panelling had been exposed.

"This little parachute, you see, is held by elastic bands, and
when it's released it shoots out and drags out the main parachute
with it. I can't show you its full size in here, of course. It's much
too long. The canopy is about sixteen feet wide."

"The little parachute is there to drag the main one out quickly?"

"Very good. Yes, that's its main purpose."

I leaned forward so fiercely that the little man recoiled. "And
does it? Has it been tested?"

"Oh, yes. Several times."

"And found to be workable?"

"Yes," Mr. Prentice said with a faint smile. "Or I wouldn't be here."

"You . . . you don't mean *you've* tested it?" I asked incredulously.

"Well, I couldn't let some young man risk his life with an untried and in some respects rather revolutionary design."

Mr. Lewis and I looked at each other, then back at the crumpled little man.

"Perhaps it is hard to believe," Mr. Prentice said. "So I've brought along some photographs."

He took out an envelope and extracted a score of photographs. They were all dated and signed on the back by the various photographers.

The first photo was an air-to-air shot, showing a bundle of old clothes falling sideways from a Sopwith three-seat biplane. "That's me," Mr. Prentice said apologetically. "You can just see the, the dragging parachute, as I call it, streaming out under the aircraft. There, see?"

"I'll be double-danged . . ."

"That was taken over the Sopwith works at Weybridge."

"Why Sopwith? Didn't you say you were with Vickers?"

"Well, you see, they wouldn't let me try it out at Vickers. Said I was too useful to them. Anyway, it was my own private project, you see, and . . . Actually I had to sneak over to Sopwith's at weekends without telling Vickers. I got Tom Sopwith to fly me."

I stared at him open-mouthed before turning back to the rest of the pictures. The first few were in sequence, from the first leap to the touch-down, though not 'all taken on the same occasion. The next was a ground shot, clearly showing Mr. Prentice drifting below the graceful canopy over a ploughed field, though at a somewhat alarming angle to the ground.

"That's the first time I sprained my ankle," he said. "I still haven't quite solved the problem of keeping the parachute completely stable. The air spills out circumferentially, you see, setting up a turbulence that tends to swing the parachute in circles as it descends."

"I've found that, too," I said faintly. "A corkscrewing effect . . ."

"Exactly. But an agile young man shouldn't have much difficulty compensating for it, on landing," Mr. Prentice said, looking at us anxiously, as if fearful that we would condemn a device that might just possibly endanger a pilot's ankles after it had saved his life.

He showed us another photograph of himself being dragged across a field on his back. "It was pretty windy that day," he said.

Mr. Lewis took a deep breath. "Mr. Prentice," he said firmly. "Would you care for some of my very best brandy?"

"Oh, no, thank you, Mr. Lewis. I'm sorry, I have an ulcer, you see."

"Bartholomew?"

"No, I've . . . given up drinking . . . Getting into training for Canada, you understand . . . But listen," I cried, turning back to Mr. Prentice, "a pack like this, even a Camel pilot could wear it easily! What do the brass say about it?"

Mr. Prentice's tale was pretty astonishing. He had first approached the authorities in July of 1917. Months went by, while he was shuffled from one department of the War Office to another, dealing with literally dozens of staff officers. Some of them had reacted to his samples and his authenticated pictures as if he were a door-to-door salesman with an inferior line of merchandise, or as if he were just another crackpot with a scheme for milking cows by electricity, or refuelling aircraft in the air, or some such impossible dream. A few of them, however, were interested enough to take a sample of his parachute, promising that it would be tested at the first opportunity.

"And?"

"They said they'd be in touch. But weeks went by, and nothing happened. When I went back again I saw a completely new set of people, and not one of them knew a thing about it. I never even got my parachute back. They just said they already had a parachute, the Calthorp design. Do you know that one, sir?"

"The Guardian Angel. It's useless."

"Yes, I'm afraid I was rather tactless and said much the same thing myself, which didn't help my cause very much. They just kept saying that the Calthorp design was the one they were committed to, and that was all there was to it."

"The man to see was the Director General of Military Aeronautics. Did you get to see him, Mr. Prentice?"

"Yes, I did finally. He was quite interested, but he also said they were interested only in the Calthorp.

"By this time, I must admit I was getting rather discouraged.

Even though a lot of people had admitted that it was superior to the Calthorp, they just kept on making excuses about not changing horses in midstream, and that sort of thing.

"Finally I decided to make one last attempt before giving up—my health was starting to suffer, you see—and go and see the Air Minister himself."

"What did the Air Minister say?"

"I don't know."

"Eh?"

"I never got to see him. I couldn't even get to meet his military aide, let alone get past him to see the Minister. It was that military aide who finally defeated me. I just couldn't go on after that."

"Some jumped-up, pompous, interfering bonehead, I've no doubt," I said bitterly. "Oh, yes, I know the type."

"M'm. As I say, I never even got to meet him. A rather odd Canadian, by all accounts."

Mr. Lewis looked up slowly.

"Wait a minute," he said. "You *are* talking about the *present* Air Minister's military aide, aren't you?"

"No, his predecessor's. Lord Rackingham."

There was a simply awful silence.

"Lord—" I began. I had to clear my throat and start again. "Lord Rackingham's military aide refused to let you see the Minister?" I faltered. "When was this?"

"Last February."

Mr. Lewis looked at me. I looked at one of Mr. Lewis' ferns.

It was I who had been the Minister's military aide at that time.

It seemed that it was I who had killed off the only good parachute design the Allies were to produce in the entire war.

There's Me, Among the Ruins

Five minutes after the rusty freighter had braked to a halt at a ruined wharf half-way along the stream, a Canadian naval lieutenant came clattering down the gangway outside my iron bedroom. He stuck his head through the hatch. The hatch was so small it looked as if it had been designed to admit only undersized deep-sea divers with the bends.

"Hey," he called in. "Where will I find this flying fella?"

I gazed up at him emaciatedly.

"Quick, man, I'm in a hurry. Which cabin is he in?"

"Flying fella?" I croaked. "That must be me. I've been flying all over this cabin for days."

"No, I mean the Flying Corps man."

"'s me."

"You're Colonel Bandy? Gee whizz."

I stood up, and immediately lurched sideways all the way across the cabin—it was a good four feet wide—and clanged against a bulkhead. My feet hadn't yet noticed that the ship had stopped yawing and pitching.

The smart young lieutenant stepped deftly into the cabin without even having the decency to smash his cranium against the top of the hatch. I was pretty annoyed at that. I'd hit it nearly every time I'd dragged my tail back from the head.

"Welcome home, sir," he said in his quick, enthusiastic voice. "My name's Toogood, port admiral's aide. Admiral Byrd-Kustard wishes me to welcome you back to Canada, Colonel, and extends an invitation to put up with him."

"Is he hard to get along with, then?" I asked numbly.

"I mean, he wants you to be his guest, during stay in Halifax." The bright-looking lieutenant stood to attention and added formally, "Him and his old lady. Okay?"

"There was some talk—" I stopped to clear my throat and scrape some rust off my voice. It had become eroded from disuse and neglect, because nobody had talked to me for such a long time; throughout most of the voyage, in fact. They'd been put off, I suppose, by the sound of my retchings, which had been echoing throughout the ship for days on end. "Some talk of my staying with the Lieutenant-Governor," I finished.

Toogood inserted eight fingers into his tunic pockets and said smoothly, "There must be some mistake, sir. We have a room all prepared for you at Admiralty House, and we're supposed to be looking after you, seeing you get to the civic reception on Friday, and so on and so forth. The admiral and his wife would be deeply disappointed if you turned them down, sir." His thumbs, hanging over the edges of his pockets, wiggled enthusiastically. "They, and in fact everybody else, are looking forward very much to meeting the hero of Morlancourt. The papers have been full of your splendid action, sir, that single handed battle against more than thirty enemy aircraft when, after all the rest of your men had been lost, you not only emerged triumphant but, in one of the most remarkable demonstrations of quick thinking, enterprise, courage, and devotion to—"

"Oh, shut up."

"Sorry," he said. "Thought you'd enjoy me piling it on. Most of our important guests can't get enough of my nauseating flattery."

"I don't mind the nauseating flattery. It's your voice I can't stand. It's so cheerful."

"I know how you feel," Lieutenant Toogood said sympathetically. "I always get seasick myself, hence my present job as the admiral's megaphone.

"We can take it, then," he added, "that you accept his invitation?"

"I guess so."

"Very good. We'll have a car waiting for you as soon as you've cleared the health authorities."

"I doubt if I will clear them. I've been at death's door for fifteen days."

"A prescription of terra firma will clear that up in no time," Toogood said briskly. "By the way, there's a few reporters waiting for you outside the dock gates."

"What, in the middle of the night?"

"It's not the middle of the night, it's broad daylight."

"It is? It's been so dark down here . . . What time is it, anyway?"

Just then, eight bells rang.

"There you are," Toogood said. "Eight bells."

"How much is eight bells?"

"Eight, of course."

"Yes," I croaked patiently. "But what time does that indicate?"

"Ah. See what you mean. Let's see, now . . . eight bells. That would be . . . Don't prompt me, now. They told me all about it at Dartmouth . . . That would be, oh—about eight in the morning?"

I gave him a look, then, clinging tightly to the nearest cock, began to draw my clothes from a rusty steampipe where they'd been hanging up to dry. I had just finished packing, wondering dully why my undies had orange streaks across them, when there was a thump of boots on the gangway outside. Somebody else was fearlessly following the naval lieutenant down to my iron maiden, laughably described by the first officer, before I boarded, as a first-class cabin amidships.

He must have meant it was first-class in comparison with the stokers' accommodation. It was amidships, all right, but so deep in the ship they had to climb *down* from the engine room to reach it.

The newcomer turned out to be a middle-aged Canadian Army captain. He peered in, looking like a speleologist who'd just discovered an unusually sordid cave.

"Is it Colonel Bandy?" he asked, panting.

"Too late, Mac," Lieutenant Toogood cried. "He's accepted the admiral's invitation."

"Damn."

The Army captain glared in through the hole. "You knew he was supposed to stay with us," he snapped.

"First come first served, Tommy."

"It's the second time in a row you've done this! It's too bad, Toogood!"

"What's all this?" I asked.

"You were supposed to stay with the Lieutenant-Governor," the captain shouted, looking at me as if I were a traitor to the country.

In fact, I'd received a very indefinite invitation, through the High Commissioner's office in Victoria Street, London, and had assumed, when the subject wasn't mentioned again, that they'd had second thoughts about it.

I tried to explain this to the Lieutenant-Governor's private secretary, Captain McCann, but he wouldn't listen. "His Honor isn't going to be very pleased when he hears you've turned down his invitation," he said loudly.

"His wife isn't, you mean," Toogood said smugly.

"What's it got to do with his wife?" I asked. Then, wearily: "Look, I'm in a sufficiently debilitated state as it is, without all this mystery. I've hardly eaten a thing for fifteen days except dog biscuits and glasses of milk," I said, "and I'm in no mood . . ." The rest died away in what sounded alarmingly like a death rattle.

"Three weeks ago, it was the Overseas Minister," McCann said, turning back to Lieutenant Toogood. "You practically kidnaped him. Now you've done it again!"

"Well, you took that famous American poet, whatsisname, off us. *And* the C-in-C, Atlantic."

"Look here," McCann demanded, glaring back at me. "Do you or do you not intend to honor your promise to stay with the Lieutenant-Governor and his wife?"

"You heard the colonel, Mac. He didn't receive a firm invitation from you—"

"I wasn't talking to you!" the Army man shouted.

The two of them continued to fume, glare, snap, and bicker for several minutes. Under the developer of their polemic, the picture gradually emerged, a trifle fuzzily, but clear enough for me to discern that it was the spouses who had issued the invitations rather than the bigwigs themselves. I gathered, with a sinking heart, that the wives had been vying with each other for some time to see who could entertain the larger number of important visitors to Halifax.

"So," I said to Toogood, after McCann had stormed back up the ladder, "you've landed me in the middle of a contest between the leading lights of Halifax society, is that it?"

"I wouldn't exactly call it a contest, sir," Toogood said cautiously.

"What would you call it, then?"

"A feud."

"Thank you. Thank you very much indeed."

Toogood waved away my thanks with a cheerful smile.

He'd been honest about it not being the middle of the night, though. Upstairs it was bright daylight.

Gratefully, I sucked in tremulous lungfuls of the first fresh air I'd imbibed since the ship had just missed colliding with Ireland, a couple of weeks ago.

A cool Maritimes breeze was competing with the hot August sun. Dockyard cranes patterned the cloudless sky. As I tottered across to the gangway, oily debris sucked and swirled between the ship's side and the battered wharf.

At the gangway, the first officer said heartily, "Well, haven't seen much of you this trip, have we?"

"And it's the last time you ever catch me on a boat again."

"Ship."

"*Or* a ship. From now on, I'll never voyage across anything wider than an old mill stream. Rotten tub . . ."

"That's no way to talk, Colonel. We gave you a cabin all to yourself, didn't we?"

"Only because there wasn't room for anybody else. There wasn't even room for me, and look how much space I take up, after fifteen days."

"M'm, you do look a trifle wasted . . . By the way, what was that Army chap in such a huff about? He stormed off the ship as if someone had called his mother a socialist."

Toogood jauntily told him about the mix-up over the invitations.

"Oh, God, are they at it again? I hope you picked the right side, Colonel. The Lieutenant-Governor's wife, Mrs. Capon, can be pretty mean when she's crossed."

"Wonderful," I said.

There was a sizeable crowd outside the docks. As I lurched through the gates, accompanied by Lieutenant Toogood, a few of them clapped, albeit a bit self-consciously.

Most of them, however, just stared, as if finding it hard to believe that this emaciated land-lubber with the face like a collapsed tent could possibly have done anything more heroic than volunteering to taste the food in an Army cookhouse.

The newspaper reporters, looking equally unimpressed, were good enough to ask pretty much the same questions as had their European confreres, so I was able to trot out the same answers without having to think too coherently.

After telling them I'd had an awful voyage, thank you, so it was doubly good to be home, I described the action once more, then settled down for the usual interrogation. This one here, with the purple stripes? A new medal, called the Distinguished Flying Cross . . . No, I hadn't heard a word about the V.C. . . . I didn't know exactly how many confirmed victories. I kept careful score the first time, but somehow the second time . . . No, not nearly as many as Billy Bishop . . . Yes, I'd met Bishop a couple of weeks ago at the Air Ministry—the greatest marksman of them all . . . No, my wife wasn't *enceinte,* and yes, I believed she was related to an earl, through her mother (that was in response to a lady reporter) . . . No, I still felt like just plain folks (liar) . . . I found the Prince of Wales charming, no hot air about him at all (the lady reporter again) . . . I didn't expect the war to end for a long time yet . . . What latest attack? . . . Oh, I hadn't heard about that, I was on the high seas at the time, and my God were they high. What happened? Don't tell me the attack was successful?

So the press interview ended with me asking them the questions, about the Australian, British, and Canadian advance on August 8, on the Amiens front, in which six German divisions had been overwhelmed, many of the German soldiers surrendering with every sign of relief and satisfaction.

"They say it's the first time that's happened in the war, the Heinies giving up so easy," the Halifax *Mail* reporter said, "and it may be the beginning of the end."

"No," I croaked authoritatively. "Don't delude yourselves, gentlemen—and lady. The war will last at least until 1920; 1920 at the very least."

When they'd finished taking pictures—Toogood managed to get into several of them in spite of my efforts to elbow him aside or stand in front of him—a naval rating drove up in a gigantic Pierce-Arrow Vestibule Suburban with brass door handles.

"We used to have a Ford Touring," Toogood said as we embedded ourselves in the upholstery, "until Mrs. Capon got her husband, the Lieutenant-Governor, to buy an American-Broc Brougham. So the admiral's wife persuaded her husband to retaliate with *this* sumptuous vehicle."

The ladies had been competing with each other for as long as he'd been in this job, Toogood said. "Mrs. Byrd-Kustard is ahead at the moment. Her last catch was the Minister for Overseas Forces, a couple of weeks ago. He was passing through Halifax on his way to London and was supposed to be staying with His Honor, Mr. Capon. But I met his train further up the line, and somehow he got the impression I was from the Lieutenant-Governor's office. By the time we had him ensconced in Admiralty House, it was too late for him to do anything about it without offending the admiral as well. Mrs. Byrd-Kustard gave me a sterling-silver mustard pot as a reward for that little *coup*."

"You should have got a good biff on the boko," I muttered.

"Sure. And I'd have deserved it, sir," Toogood said in that disarming way of his. "But what else can I do? I'd lose my job if I displeased the old girl, and I'm sure as hell not in any hurry to get back to my proper job, getting seasick on over-age destroyers, if I can help it."

I could understand that, anyway.

"Even so," he went on, drawing down a silk shade to keep out the sun, "our *coups* barely make up for Mrs. Capon's last triumph, when she not only lured the admiral's own superior officer to the Lieutenant-Governor's mansion, but organized a state dinner for him, knowing that Mrs. Byrd-Kustard was down with the flu.

"Mind you, Mrs. Byrd-Kustard attended the dinner anyway, and deliberately breathed germs all over Mrs. Capon. Their husbands have tried to persuade the ladies to share important guests on a rota basis, but they're too far gone in enmity for that. It's quite painful to see the way they smile at each other whenever they meet by accident."

"What are they like?"

"Mrs. Capon is like an aging actress who isn't getting enough good parts. Though, come to think of it," he added thoughtfully, "she already has two or three good parts . . . As for Mrs. Byrd-Kustard, she's like one of those lamplighters' poles: long and thin, with a flicker of flame at the top.

"Oh, yes," he added, "and she hates to be touched."

"Touched? Ah, I see. You mean she's totally unreceptive to appeals to sentiment, and cannot abide romantic or tender exchanges of any sort."

"Eh?"

"I'm explaining what you meant. That there is a certain cynicism to her outlook, and cloying sentimentality is abhorrent to her basically realistic attitude to life. That's what you meant, isn't it?"

"I just meant she hates to be touched, Colonel."

"That's what I just said, wasn't it?"

"Oh, forget it," Toogood said.

We were half-way to Admiralty House before I remembered to feel the exhilaration of the returning traveller.

It was over two years since I had left. As we drove through the narrow streets under the squinting sun, I gazed at the dingy Victorian edifices with gratitude and some emotion.

I even found the sound of the trams affecting, as they screeched and swayed around the telegraph-tangled corners, and the clop and groan of the slovens that plodded over the cobbles, loaded with barrels, sacks, and cloth-capped drivers.

Although the grey city of Halifax was more like a British than a Canadian port, there was still enough of a difference to make it feel like the threshold of home, particularly the accents, the cleaner air, and the bustling, optimistic pace. The most gratifying impression, though, even in that huddled town, was the sense of space. In Europe, everything seemed so crowded and constricted, with no room to move on the sidewalks, and little feeling of elbow room, even in the small towns; and always the sense that beyond the next hill was another crowded place. When I caught my first glimpse of the glorious sweep of forested horizon beyond the Bedford Basin, and sensed the scale of the land beyond it, I felt relief and freedom. This really was where I belonged, after all.

"Home," I croaked, taking a deep, proud breath of Narrows mud, rotting fish-heads, oxy-acetylene smoke, and the pong from the refinery near McNab's Island. "Even if it does look a bit run-down." I cleared my throat noisily. "The docks look as if they've been bombed. And all these boarded-up windows—is there a shortage of glass or something?"

"That was the explosion."

"Eh? Oh, yes . . ." I said, looking around again. "I heard about that."

"You'll hear little else while you're here. People are still talking about it, nine months later."

"A munitions ship, wasn't it?"

"Last December. The *Mont Blanc*. It was loaded with TNT. Another ship ran into it. When it went up, it damaged towns sixty miles away." Toogood's two gold rings gleamed in the sun as he turned to point at Citadel Hill. "It was only the hill that saved the whole city from being devastated. You should see the north end of town. It's completely destroyed. They still don't know how many people were killed. Over a thousand five hundred, anyway."

The car bounced and rumbled as it sped along a cobbled street between hordes of sunburned girls on bicycles, all shamelessly showing their ankles. We passed what had once been a row of wooden houses, their walls leaning, splintered and scorched.

"The *Mont Blanc* was also carrying benzol, and it rained fire for minutes on end. Houses were still burning in the snow three days later."

As we reached the centre of town and were puttering slowly along crowded Barrington Street, a car came racing down one of the steep intersecting streets, its horn parp-parping urgently. Toogood and I watched uneasily as it hurtled toward us at a reckless pace, the front wheels wiggling wildly. It was being driven by a woman.

She looked remarkably unconcerned, even though her vehicle was about to plough into the side of one of the trams. The tram, as if in anticipation, was already screeching. Beside her in the swaying vehicle was a maid, who, to make up for her mistress' unconcern, was looking distinctly apprehensive.

At the last moment, the tall, narrow vehicle swung away from the tram, rising perilously on two wheels as it did so. Missing a pair of gentlemen in black serge by a good eight inches, it screeched to a halt transversely across the prow of our Pierce-Arrow.

One of the black-serge gentlemen shouted angrily and shook his fist. A helmeted policeman started portentously toward the offending vehicle, but stopped when he caught sight of the driver. He turned away to tie his bootlace. When nobody was looking, he hurried up the nearest alleyway.

"Mrs. Capon," Toogood murmured.

The lady's face, now seen to be slightly flushed, was only about six feet away. Toogood leaned over to open the window on my side. Simultaneously Mrs. Capon flung open the high, narrow door of her brougham, just as a cloth-capped cyclist was shooting between the two cars. He ran into the door and fell under the mudguard with a cry of alarm, his wheels spinning and scraping.

"Do look where you're going," Mrs. Capon cried irritably, projecting remarkably well over the din of bicycle bells, grinding trams, hooting cars, and pedestrian exclamations.

The cyclist stared up groggily from under the mudguard. Mrs. Capon paid no further attention to him, but addressed us across the six-foot gap.

"I thought it was you, you hooligan," she said in her extremely loud voice. "I thought I recognized your motor car, and I said to myself if that's that son-of-a-bitch Toogood, I want a little word with him."

Beside her, the maid whimpered at this shocking language, but for some reason covered her nose rather than her ears.

"Oh, do stop blubbering, Olive," Mrs. Capon exclaimed impatiently.

"I've banged me nose, Mam."

"Well, you should know to hang on properly," Mrs. Capon shouted. She had a Canadian accent, garnished with Irish, delivered through a slack mouth that didn't quite cover several dangerous-looking teeth. Though she was expensively attired in a light silk dress, there was a certain air of dishevelment about her. A tendril of Celtic hair hung from under her theatrical hat.

"Always delighted to have a little word with you, Mrs. Capon," Toogood called back, touching his cap in a rather nervous salute.

She pushed the door wide open for a better view. "You won't be so delighted when I've finished with you," she shouted. "I've just this minute heard from Captain McCann, and I was just on my way to tell that woman just what I thought of her. But now I've seen you, Mr. so-called Toogood, I'll give *you* a piece of my mind instead. I'm going to ask my husband to lodge an official complaint about your conduct, you gold-ringed maggot. You've done this sort of thing once too often, my lad, and I've half a mind . . ."

The rest was lost in an outburst of hooting and raving from a growing line of frustrated drivers behind us. A fair crowd of morning shoppers were also clustering at the street corner, whispering and nudging. Even the seagulls seemed excited by the *brouhaha*, as they planed and complained over the rooftops.

Mrs. Capon's castigations continued under the uproar, most of her words being inaudible, which was probably just as well, as there were several sailors nearby, as well as a gang of urchins.

Her voice bridged a lull in the vehicular racket. ". . . not going to get away with it this time, my fine featherbrained friend," she hollered. "Even if he is only half a colonel." Her little green eyes, arranged on a stave of wrinkles, flicked suddenly to me. "That's you, is it?" she asked scornfully.

"I'm really sorry about this, Mrs. Capon," I wheedled hoarsely. "But honest, I didn't realize it was a definite invitation from the—"

"Some warrior you are, letting yourself be bullied into staying with that stuck-up length of drainpipe," she interrupted. "Well, all I can say is, don't expect any help or favors from the Lieutenant-Governor. And don't expect us to attend your reception either. Seeing you now, it'll probably be as dull as ditchwater anyway."

There was a lot more of this, but we missed most of it because of a renewed bedlam of bellowing and parping. By now, the traffic behind us was backed up as far as the Bedford Basin.

That didn't seem to trouble Mrs. Capon in the least. "Anyway, I've read all about you between the lines," she shouted across the gap between the two cars. "And you're no great catch anyway. From what I've heard about you, and by God your face confirms it, her ladyship'll be sorry she ever landed you, that's all I've got to say. And another thing: I remember you were in the papers a few months ago as well, about some half-witted speech you made about Sir Douglas Haig. I wonder if her ladyship knows about that." Her voice went all upper-class British. "She just *adores* dear Sir Douglas." Her flushed face rearranged itself again into a scowl. "Maybe I'll tell her and she can find out what kind of a snake-in-the-grass she's landed, you simpering carthorse. Good day to you, *Colonel* Bandy."

So saying, she slammed the door and backed her electric car rapidly out of the way of the southbound traffic, scattering pedestrians as she did so. A moment later, she was shooting back up the hill again, on the wrong side of the street.

"Trifle fiery, isn't she?" I whined, as we drove on. "Gee, I certainly wouldn't want to get in *her* bad books."

After a wash and brush-up in a room that was as chilly, even in August, as it was overfurnished—it contained a huge hearts-of-oak bed with about fourteen layers of bedclothes, all of them damp—I came downstairs to meet the other half of the feud.

As I was crossing the panelled hall, past an artistically arranged display of naval mementos, battle standards, musical instruments, and the like, I heard her saying in precise but approving terms, ". . . done splendidly, Toogood. That will teach her to confiscate the admiral's very own superior officer, right from under our noses. She was furious, was she? Wonderful. You must tell me all about it."

She broke off as I rolled, Jolly Jack Tar-like, into the Admiralty House drawing room.

"Ah, Colonel," she said regally as I approached, wearing my upper-class face. "How very pleased we are that you were able to accept our invitation. Welcome to Admiralty House."

Toogood's description hadn't been overly exaggerated. Mrs. Byrd-Kustard was very nearly as tall as I was, and even thinner, with fanatic eyes and a nose you could have used as a cheese-cutter. She held herself as if her stays were made of reinforcing rods.

She looked a good deal more rigid a moment later. This was after I'd lurched forward to seize her flipper, and wring it as if pumping out the bilges of a side dragger.

"Darned glad to meet you, Mrs. Byrd-Kustard," I exclaimed enthusiastically. A moment later I was forced to seize her shoulder as the drawing-room floor heaved like the deck of a 70-gun ship of the line off Ushant.

"Sorry," I said, shifting my grip to her forearm until the house had settled itself on an even keel. "Still a bit unsteady on the pins, you understand."

Mrs. Byrd-Kustard had suddenly developed lockjaw—all over. There definitely seemed to be some sort of internal struggle going on there.

However, after swallowing a few times and taking several quick, shallow breaths, she managed to say, "Yes . . . Well . . . perhaps you'd better be seated," and showed me how to do it by dropping onto a *chaise-longue*, suddenly, as if someone had just kicked her behind the knees.

I looked around for a seat. She immediately arranged the folds of her dress to each side of her, to make it plain that I was not expected to plonk myself beside her.

"Toogood," she said in an unnaturally high voice, "would you hurry and inform the admiral that Colonel Bandy has arrived."

Toogood murmured and withdrew, glancing back a trifle anxiously as he did so.

After a while, Mrs. Byrd-Kustard began to regain her color.

"As I say, my husband and I are pleased you were able to accept our invitation to stay with us for several—for a day or so," she said, watching me through perceptibly narrowed eyes as I felt my way into the nearest upholstered receptacle. "We're looking forward very keenly indeed to hearing all about that heroic exploit of yours, against the Heathen Hun."

We smiled at each other. It was hate at first sight.

"It was nothing really," I said. Mrs. Byrd-Kustard nodded approvingly at this correctly modest response. "It was merely," I went on, "a typical example of my brilliant flying, shooting skill, quick thinking, opportunism, and outright panic."

I settled myself more comfortably into the armchair. "Though in fact," I said, "all I was doing was looking after my own skin."

Mrs. Byrd-Kustard didn't seem to like things like skin being mentioned. "There must have been a little more to it than that, Colonel," she said, steepling her fingers. They were trembling only slightly, now. "For I believe you had the honor to be personally congratulated by none other than Sir Douglas Haig himself."

"I'm not sure whether he congratulated me or not," I said with an equally hypocritical smile. "His Chief of Intelligence introduced me, but all I heard from the field marshal was a grunt."

"Indeed? That's strange. I remember him as invariably expressing himself very clearly indeed."

"Who? *Haig?*"

"But if in fact his response was a trifle lacking in clarity or enthusiasm," she said, smiling in a way that suggested she was receiving an enema, "perhaps he also was beginning to doubt whether all he had read in the papers was true."

Touché, thought I. "As Haig is responsible for half the lies published in the papers," I said, flexing my own *épée,* "I should hope he *would* have some doubts."

"I happen to know personally," she said, sitting even more erect, were that possible—and it weren't—"that Sir Douglas is a man of the utmost honesty and integrity."

"So was Czar Nicholas the Second, and look what's happened to him."

"I met him and his charming wife before the war," she said, as if I hadn't spoken, "when he was commander in chief at Aldershot."

It was no good. She was obviously one of those who preferred to see war in Tennysonian terms, rather than in those of, say, Siegfried Sassoon.

"Oh, yeah?" I said.

"We were invited more than once to his select dinner parties, and I must confess I developed a particular admiration for his methodical qualities and attention to detail. You only had to see him on the fairway to realize that. My husband played golf with him, and told me all about it later: the infinite pains Sir Douglas took over every single stroke—bringing to that game those qualities of dedication and painstaking care that have since made him such a success as commander in chief in France. My husband was so impressed, he has never played since."

It seemed like hours before the admiral joined us. He came in rapidly, puffing distractedly at a cigarette. I arose, with almost as much alacrity as relief. Unfortunately, the sudden motion caused me to lurch slightly, the result, as before, of fifteen days of nautical disequilibrium.

Mrs. Byrd-Kustard flinched. It was almost as if she thought I might grab her again to support myself—perhaps this time by the throat.

"Ah," the admiral said, after Toogood had performed the introductions. "So this is the young aviator whose heroic exploits have so enlivened the pages of the newspapers of late."

"Yes, that's me all right," I said, essaying a light laugh. It came out like the rattle of an anchor chain.

The admiral started slightly, and puffed more furiously than ever at his dog-end. I looked at him in some surprise.

All the admirals I'd met at the Air Ministry had autocratic beaks and ferocious voices. Admiral Byrd-Kustard, however, had a squashy sort of nose, and tended to mumble, a fault that had led to some confusion on the bridge of his last ship. A remark to the effect that a passing seagull was a "speedy tern" had been interpreted as an order for full speed astern, with the result that his battleship had run into a lighthouse; hence his present job in this outpost of the Empire.

"We've been having a most interesting conversation, Bertram," his wife said. She seemed to be making some kind of signal to him. "Especially about our acquaintanceship with dear Sir Douglas."

"Oh, God, yes," the admiral said. Whatever her signal meant, he didn't seem to understand it either. He puffed hurriedly at his cigarette again, and winced as his upper lip sizzled. "You must tell us all about your exploit, Bandy," he mumbled. I opened my mouth to do so. "Perhaps at dinner tomorrow night. We're having one or two people in. I'm sure they'll be most interested to hear all about it first hand."

His initial wave of enthusiasm had already drained away into the scuppers. When nobody said anything for a few seconds, he looked longingly toward the decanters.

His wife said quickly, "I suppose you'll be looking forward eagerly to seeing your parents again, Colonel."

"Yes, Ma'am. I'll be leaving for Ottawa right after the reception on Friday."

"Oh, splendid," Mrs. Byrd-Kustard exclaimed, smilingly genuinely for the first time that morning.

The admiral started chunnering again. I couldn't make out what he was saying, and had an impulse to call out sharply, "Speak up, man, you're not on your battleship now!" But having failed dismally to earn his wife's approval, I was all the more anxious to recoup the situation by making the best possible impression on the admiral; so I just said, "Eh?"

"Toogood says you bumped into Mrs. Capon on the way over."

"That scandalous woman," Mrs. Byrd-Kustard said. "The Lieutenant-Governor would have got rid of her long ago had he not his position to think of. What a common person she is. She is a disgrace to Halifax society. Mrs. Cross tells me she created a most disagreeable scene at the flower show last Wednesday, stumbling over a display of the Honorable Mr. Harvard's prize gladioli. So we will not discuss her if you don't mind, Bertram. Others may gossip about her abandoned behavior and deplorable habits, but we must be above that sort of thing."

"Mumble," the admiral said.

In the leaden silence that followed, he glanced around distractedly. Seeing no empty glasses, he said, "Toogood, this isn't very hospitable of you. What about a spot of sherry for our guest?"

"No!"

We all turned and looked wide-eyed at Mrs. Byrd-Kustard.

"That is . . . isn't it a little early in the day for that, Bertram?"

"Oh, is it?"

42

A moment later, I caught her shooting urgent frowns at him again—and darting her eyes in my direction.

It was only then I understood why she'd been looking at me with such suspicion since I first floundered into her drawing room.

It was all that swaying about I'd been doing, because my legs still didn't believe they were on dry land again.

She thought I'd been tanking up at some dockside groggery.

Another View of Halifax

Dinner the following evening, attended by some of the poshest people in Halifax, was initially something of a strain. Mrs. Byrd-Kustard not only remained convinced that I was addicted to alcohol but had obviously had a word with the servants about my problem, with the result that when I signalled for a second glass of wine, they avoided my vicinity with such badly acted preoccupation that some of the guests also began to regard me warily, as if I might at any moment pull up my pant legs and start tap-dancing on the sherry trifle, or drool into the nearest cleavage. But I would never have done that. There were no cleavages around. The ladies all wore gowns determinedly secured at the throat.

However, I wasn't going to let a little misunderstanding get me down, so to show that I was as sober as anyone, I launched into a suave, polished, but restrained account of my nautical adventures, as befitted the dignified occasion; and in fact held the company spellbound for nigh on twenty minutes with my tales of the sea.

"The sea" (the old salt related) "more than lived up to its reputation as the bounding main. It wouldn't have been so bad if the Atlantic had been battering along anywhere near the Plimsoll line, but the ship was riding so high even some of the barnacles were sticking out of the water."

I looked around brightly. Everybody was listening most attentively, without even blinking. After a moment, Mrs. Byrd-Kustard said faintly, "Surely that's not possible, is it, Bertram?"

"I assure you, Ma'am," I said. "We were returning empty, you see. Our only ballast was a few tons of brine that poured in when the seacook opened the seacocks somewhere off Saltee. That's in Ireland," I explained to a little old lady who was listening in a catatonic sort of way. "They said the seacook was demented, you know. I thought he was behaving very sensibly."

As the guests sat there in rapt silence, I leaned back in a lordly fashion, pleased to hear that my voice had returned to its normal, piquant whine. "It was just as well there was nobody on board with artistic pretensions," I said, "for my green face must have clashed revoltingly with the ocean blue. Quite apart from all the wallowings, which prevented me from keeping anything down except several litres of saliva, I hardly slept for more than nine and a half minutes at a time."

There was a faint clink as somebody pushed away his pudding.

"This was mainly because the marine noises keep changing every hour on the hour. I was enclosed in an iron cabin deep in the ship —I'm sure it was below the bilge, Admiral—and I'd just be getting used to one aural rhythm—the rusty grindings of the engine, the beatings of the generator, the gurgling of the bilgewater, the ravings of the cook, and so forth—and would be drifting off into a dehydrated slumber when, after exactly one hour, the rhythm would alter itself in some subtle way, just enough to drag one back to wild-eyed wakefulness. The machinery would still be thumping away, of course, but now it would be grinding its teeth as well; the pumps might still be clanking, but with a greater urgency; or the hum of the air-conditioning might die away altogether, to be replaced by queer tearing and spashing noises, as if corpses were being slid into the sea down nail-studded planks.

"By then I was so debilitated that my uniform looked as if there were nobody in it; so starved, parched, dazed, battered, and feeble as to make even retching a formidable but not entirely inefficacious effort.

"And that," I said, "was only my second day out."

After a moment, the admiral said, "Weren't you supposed to be staying with the Lieutenant-Governor?"

I'd been particularly anxious to make a good impression that evening, because, as well as being convinced that I was a common drunk, Mrs. Byrd-Kustard had also got it into her head that I was also a common lecher.

What had happened was this: that morning I'd been taken in charge by the mayor's wife, who, as if under the impression that I was the head of a trade delegation, had dispatched me on a tour of Halifax industry: steel mills, biscuit and confectionery factories, and a fish-curing plant; and, in the afternoon, on a sightseeing trip through the worst parts of Halifax, to see the damage.

She had organized these activities through a women's club. I spent about seven grueling hours in the company of dozens of twittering ladies, every one of whom had her own personal anecdote to relate about The Great Explosion. One had seen a horse and cart flying over her house. Another, a Mrs. McAndrews, had been blown out of bed and had hit the ceiling. "My," she said, wide-eyed, "you should just see the great dent I made in my bedroom ceiling."

She was one of the good-looking ones. "Can that be arranged?" I whispered, under suggestively arched eyebrows. She looked pretty flustered at that, and for the rest of the tour had remained hidden behind some of the burlier members of the throng.

I'd only said it for fun, of course, and to relieve a momentary boredom. In fact I'd been almost as taken aback as she was. It hadn't sounded like me at all. I couldn't help wondering at the changes that had come over me since leaving the country twenty-five months before with a moral outlook that would have made John Knox seem a dirty old man by comparison. Now look at me: flirting with comely widows.

The trouble was, Mrs. McAndrews was among those who had been invited back to Admiralty House for tea, and she had told my hostess about it instead of keeping decently quiet, the bitch.

So, even before dinner, Mrs. Byrd-Kustard's manner had been pretty arctic. To top it off, and entirely ruining the memorable impression I'd made during that monologue of mine, as we were strolling back to the drawing room, I tottered again.

I'd just finished congratulating myself on once again re-establishing a working relationship with the earth, too. Mind you, it was a very minor totter, hardly more than a teeter, in fact, and normally it wouldn't have been noticed by anyone who wasn't on the lookout for further symptoms of inebriation and debauchery.

Unfortunately, in tottering (or teetering), my foot clacked against the bottom exhibit of the admiral's artful display of fifes, drums, and battle-tattered ensigns salvaged from some of the Royal

Navy's more notable defeats. The whole works came down with a reverberating crash. But that wasn't the worst of it. I had to grab at somebody for support, and of all people, it would have to be Mrs. Byrd-Kustard.

The result was so awful that I had split nerve-ends for the next twenty-four hours. She uttered a piercing scream in which fright and fury were so mixed as to be inseparable outside of a psychoanalytical centrifuge, were there such an apparatus. Turning on me with gritted eyes and staring teeth, she clawed at my hands with nails that I'm sure had been specially sharpened for the occasion.

Everybody stood transfixed, nay, petrified, all their muscles bunched up like cauliflowers. There was not a sound, except for the patter of blood from my lacerated veins, and the ticking of a side drum as it rolled across the floor. We all watched blindly, until it had settled down with a final, wincing clunk.

It really didn't seem worthwhile explaining that I hadn't quite got my land legs yet.

Not more than ten minutes after the last guest had departed in disorder, I accidentally overheard her talking on the telephone to her arch-enemy, the Lieutenant-Governor's wife. Well, I didn't exactly overhear by accident—I emerged from cover to listen the moment I heard my name mentioned.

"No, no, not at all, Mrs. Capon," Mrs. Byrd-Kustard was saying. She was holding the telephone receiver as if it had recently fallen in the exercise yard of a dog pound. "He's a most delightful person, quite dashing, with a most stimulating way of describing his experiences. The admiral was just saying to me that Colonel Bandy was a most . . . Yes, I realize we've had our little differences in the past, and that's what I'm calling about, Mrs. Capon. I do feel we have an obligation to set an example— noblesse oblige, as they say—and much as we should like to keep him, one cannot help but feel a certain moral obligation to . . . Would that be possible? Oh, thank God—that would be . . . a splendid start to a new era in our relationship, don't you . . . ? . . . Oh, no, not at all. As I say, he's a most intriguing man, quite overwhelming in fact, and we're *most* reluctant to part with him, but I really do think it's high time we ended this undignified conflict that . . ."

Anyway, it was *much* more comfortable at Mrs. Capon's.

At first Mrs. Capon's manner was not particularly cordial. In fact, she seemed to view the transfer with a good deal of suspicion. I wondered uneasily how long it would take some busybody to whisper the reason Mrs. Byrd-Kustard had suddenly become so terribly reasonable and unselfish.

It took about three and a half hours. To my surprise, when Mrs. Capon heard the gossip her eyes lit up like headlights.

"Why didn't you tell me you were a common drunkard?" she cried gayly, after lunch. "Why, I'd have been much more friendly this morning if I'd known."

"But I hardly drink at all, Mrs. Capon."

She laughed as if I were joshing her.

"Admittedly I was starting to imbibe rather too much in France, but ever since then—"

"I know," she said, touching my arm and smiling at me approvingly. "Captain McCann's told me all about you getting fuddled at their swank dinner last night, and talking wildly about vomit."

"But I was stone cold sober!"

"Oh, sure. That's why you smashed all their hall furniture and clawed at Mrs. Byrd-Kustard's corsets."

"I *didn't!* I—"

"Oh, I'd have just loved to have seen her ladyship's face when she discovered you were a confirmed boozer. So that's why the old trout was being so accommodating. Well, don't you worry, son, I'm not one to look down on a fellow just because he's a thorough souse."

"But I'm not! I—"

"I'm not averse to a spot myself now and again," she said, and, after a quick glance around, poured each of us about eleven fingers of rum. She drank half of hers in one go. "And what's this I hear about you forcing your way into Mrs. McAndrews' bedroom and getting so enthralled with her that half the ceiling falls onto the bed?"

"Good grief, does everyone in Halifax know what everyone else is doing?"

"Yes—you dirty bugger," she said, giving me a sly nudge and a remarkably coarse wink.

"Honest, Mrs. Capon, it wasn't like that at all," I protested, just as the Lieutenant-Governor came in with Captain McCann and found me clutching a glass so brimming with rum that the slightest tremor sent rivulets of the stuff coursing down my ivory knuckles.

A distinguished-looking gentleman, much aware of the dignity of his position, Mr. Capon was not at all pleased to find us busily transfusing alcohol at two in the afternoon. He looked bitterly at his wife. The poor woman almost cringed, obviously only too aware that she wasn't good enough for him.

After confiscating the bottle, he took me aside and said, "I hope you don't mind my saying this, Colonel, but I wish you wouldn't encourage my wife to imbibe quite so early in the day."

"But I—"

"Please don't think I fail to understand. The hardships of war, and so forth. I know a little of the appalling conditions at the front, the bottle frequently being your only recourse and comfort."

"No, 'tisn't, Your Honor. I—"

"But as you may already have gathered, my wife also tends to look for solace in that quarter, with not nearly as much excuse."

"But I—"

"Well, we won't say any more about it," he said, ordering his quadrate muscle to deliver a tolerant smile to his lower lip. It made him look as if he were auditioning for the part of Dracula. "Mrs. Capon is a cross I have to bear, but all I ask is that you not add a further burden by giving way to your own alcoholic tendencies."

God, being back at school couldn't have been any worse.

That evening, the Premier of the Province and an Honorable or two of the Legislative Council came to dinner. Either they were unmarried or word had gotten out that I was an unprincipled cad, for their wives failed to turn up.

That was one difference between North America and Europe, I thought. In Europe, hearing I was a sex-maniac, the women would have come to dinner in droves.

As soon as Mr. Capon and his visitors had retired to the study for some political haggling (taking the brandy with them), Mrs. Capon sashayed into her private sitting room at the back of the house, and after firmly closing the door and cutting off my escape, took a fresh bottle of rum from behind Law Society Volume XIV.

I hurriedly started yawning, stretching, and mumbling excuses about being a trifle weary. As it was still only half after eight, my excuses weren't overly convincing.

"What's the matter with you? You don't want me to think you're reluctant to keep me company, do you? Come on, sit down and stop babbling. Anyone would think you were a damned Temperancer instead of an old soak, the way you're going on. Here, that's not enough to drown a flea. Pour us a decent snort, will you, for God's sake. That's more like it, now."

I suppose, being rather more determined than I used to be, I could have acted firmly, and told her that I'd no wish to reel around with her in drunken debauchery this particular evening. Unfortunately, feeling sorry for somebody invariably immobilized my shindy instincts. Besides, I was more than normally anxious to avoid any kind of scene, and still determined to make a good impression on my fellow countrymen, especially people like Capon, on whose peacetime influence I might one day have to rely; if I survived to call upon it, that is.

So I just sat there in a sulk. This made Mrs. Capon tremendously friendly.

"You're a man after my own heart," she said, leaning over unsteadily and squeezing my arm. "I knew it the minute I clapped eyes on you. You don't belong either, do you, even if you are half a colonel. It's because you're not smart enough to show the bastards respect when they don't deserve it. Whereas with me, it's because I've been too smart. I've shot up the elevator of life so fast I've passed my own floor—the one where all the commercial travellers are, and freight agents and publicans and the like . . ."

She was sloshing back the rum as if another Great Explosion was due at midnight—and it probably was. As for me, it was a good job I'd had a good dinner that evening, to help soak up the liquor. Even so, after two of her snorts my eyes seemed intent on swishing sideways and lodging somewhere behind my ears. I was looking around desperately for somewhere to pour the stuff when she wasn't looking.

The only convenient receptacle anywhere near my chair was a Singer Sewing Machine. It had five drawers, two of which were within easy reach. I wondered if they would be sufficiently leakproof.

I could hardly check to make sure, though. "Pardon me, but are your drawers leakproof?" No.

Gosh, though, I had to do something. If the Lieutenant-Governor and his mates came in and found me genuinely blotto, I'd lose what little reputation I still had in these parts.

I was really dismayed at the mess I was making on the doorstep of home. It was no good telling myself defensively that everybody seemed to have a surplus of decorum and a deficit of humor. I ought to have remembered that, however worthy your average Canadian was, a gay, light-hearted, abandoned attitude to life was not one of his attributes.

Somehow I had to salvage the last remnants of my reputation before they got to hear about it in Ottawa, and started cancelling all the free dinners. I considered letting my hand drop casually to the floor and pouring the fire-water into the imitation Axminster. But then visualized the Lieutenant-Governor coming in and seeing a wet patch under my chair. He would almost certainly conclude that I was incontinent as well as alcoholic.

The simple fact was, there was only one feasible place to dispose of the rum, as an alternative to admitting I'd had enough and causing a scene. And Mrs. Capon certainly knew how to cause a scene. So, watching her carefully—at the moment, she was staring resentfully at the wallpaper, a dense, vinous design with bamboo trellises, calculated to drive *anyone* to drink—I inserted two fingers into my left boot, to pull the leather away from my trousers, and, with a heavy heart, poured the rum into the gap thus created.

Only just in time, too. Mrs. Capon was looking at me again, her lips sagging away from her formidable teeth.

"Have you ever been to Ireland?" she was asking.

"I once went there by mistake," I said dejectedly, feeling the liquor soaking my sock.

This statement failed to rouse any interest, except as a stepping stone into her own stream of thought. "I came to Canada by mistake," she mumbled.

"Oh, yes?"

"My father abandoned the family when I was thirteen, and came out here, leaving us to fend for ourselves. But, a couple of years later, he wrote to my sister Siobhan—she was always his favorite, the green-eyed cow—asking her to join him and look after the house for him.

"But he got our names mixed up, you see, and I came instead. Father wasn't at all pleased, I can tell you, specially as he hadn't the ready cash to send me back, even though he was a puisne judge at the time and getting all of six thousand dollars a year."

"M'm, most judges do seem to be puny and undersized," I said, wiggling my toes dispiritedly.

"Puisne, you daft bugger. P-u-i- . . . whatever the sod it is. That's how I met my husband, Mr. Capon. He was up in court for reckless driving at twelve miles an hour along the public highway.

"I only married him," she said, swishing her rum around, "because he was going to have a baby."

"Ah. Eh?"

"He'd given it to his private secretary."

"What, Captain McCann?"

"Oooh, don't be so silly. How could Captain McCann have a baby? His secretary, you great carthorse. My husband was at-torney-general of Nova Scotia then, and in line for this job, so he couldn't afford a scandal. So the idea was I'd marry him and take over her baby."

"About my remark about Captain McCann," I said firmly, "I naturally didn't think *he* was capable of having a baby, I just thought you meant he intended to hand—"

"Pass us your glass, for God's sake, and stop interruptin'. Any-way, it turned out she wasn't having a baby after all, and I was stuck with an attorney-general, when I could have married a publican . . . Tom Swift his name was . . . Oh, he was lovely . . . chest like a barrel of ale, eyes like two bungs . . ."

Two tears coursed down her right cheek. The other, for some reason, remained dry.

"Made the best whisky in Truro, he did, until the government caught him for back taxes . . ."

I was in a pretty unhappy state by the time the second glassful of rum had gone into my boot. I'd paid several quid for those boots in London. I tried not to think what it was doing to the leather. I'd probably turn up at the civic reception tomorrow with one brilliantly polished boot and one crinkled like a corrugated shed.

Now she was commiserating with herself. "I've no friends, do you know that?" She glared at me as if it were my fault. "I've no friends!"

"No friends. I see."

52

"I'm too low for His bloody Honor's acquaintances and too high for the ones I'd like to know. Nobody invites me to their homes any more, since I was sick on Mrs. Graham's cat. Is it any wonder me only consolation is the demon rum?"

"You're not drinking," she said suddenly.

"I am. Look, my glass is empty, Mrs.—"

"Well, you don't look like you're drinking to me."

"I'll drink to you anytime, Mrs. Capon," I said gallantly.

"You don't look like a boozer, either. What are you, some sort of fake?"

I had to pour us another drink before she would calm down again. That emptied the bottle.

I raised my glass, trying to look as if I were having a real beano. Luckily her eyes glazed over long enough for me to get the glass into position for the next insertion into my boot.

"Tell me a confish," she said.

"What?"

"Tell me one of your con—confidences and I'll tell you one of mine."

"You mean, tell you a secret?"

"Don't you understand plain English? Tell m' one y'r confish, and I'll tell one, one of mine . . ."

"Ah. Well, let me see, now."

"You know what? My father's letter to Siobhan. He didn't get the names mixed up at all. I instep—intercepted's letter, and let on it was me he wanted. Tha's how I came to Canada. There. Never told anyone else that. I ins—insepted his letter, an', an', know what?"

"What?"

"I made him think he'd made a mistake with the names, see. Oh, I was always the smart one, right enough . . ."

"M'm. Well, I think I'll go to bed now," I said firmly.

"Shaddup and siddown. What's . . . what's happened to your drink?" She glared at me accusingly. "I din't see you drink that drink. You know what you are? You're a hypocrite. Don't believe you're a drunk after all."

"You're the only person in Halifax who doesn't, then," I said gloomily, feeling the rum sloshing between my toes. God, how did I always get myself into these situations? Captain Blackbourne would never have been mistaken for a chronic drunk. Derby would never have poured rum into his boots. Why was it always I that was forced to do things like that?

It was my face, that's what it was. I should have gone to that plastic surgeon of Carson's. If I'd looked like Katherine's brother Robert, with his strong, uncomplicated physiognomy, I would never have been suspected of being an habitué of low taverns, or of raping members of the Women's Guild. But my huge face, with its expanse of bland incredulity, invariably caused others to believe the worst of me. Dogs barked instinctively, parrots bit me, children kicked me, senior officers instantly diagnosed dumb insolence, and little old ladies hit me with brollies; whereas I was really the most normal fellow it was possible to meet, utterly temperate in manner, attitude, habit, and outlook.

The whole situation was enraging. Then, suddenly, it was alarming again, when I heard the door to the Lieutenant-Governor's study open, and voices sound in the hall. He had concluded his business. Any moment, now, he would enter and find both of us sitting in a stupor, hers alcoholic, mine of despairing fury at the sheer injustice of it all.

With abrupt, teeth-gritted resolution, I got up and started for the door, my boot squelching hideously, as if I had one foot in a cowshed.

"Where you going?" Mrs. Capon mumbled.

"Bathroom!" I hissed viciously, and peered out into the hall. The Lieutenant-Governor was in the doorway of the study, chatting to his cronies.

The telephone rang inside the study. As soon as Capon had gone to answer it, I charged toward the circular staircase and shot up as if pursued by shrieking chimeras, and scuttled into my room, where I hurriedly removed the boot from my drenched foot, poured the rum into the only available receptacle, a certain domestic utensil usually kept under the bed, and wrung out my sock, then stood and screamed and cursed silently in the middle of the room, jumping up and down and flailing my arms, and imagining myself with a broadsword, laying into everybody I'd met in Halifax, chopping off heads wholesale, and Mrs. Capon's twice over.

The worst of it was, I really needed a drink, now.

Half an hour later, I was still sitting on the bed in my bare feet, mumbling and softly pounding the bed post with my fist, when there was a tap at the door, and a maid came in and said timidly that His Honor would like to see me in his study as soon as possible.

I marched truculently into the study, expecting to be blamed, after all, for getting his wife drunk again. But after a searching glance to make sure I was sufficiently in control of myself to take in what he had to say, he spoke on an entirely different subject.

"You were leaving for Ottawa tomorrow night, weren't you, Bandy? After the civic reception?"

"Yes."

"I'm afraid you'll have to change your plans. I've just had a call from Ottawa. The Prime Minister is arriving tomorrow. He wants to meet you."

"He's coming to Halifax just to see me? Gee."

"Of course he isn't. He has several engagements in Nova Scotia next week. He's the Honorable Member for Halifax."

"Oh."

"But the reason I've summoned you, Bandy, is that . . . well, Sir Robert is to be my guest during his sojourn in Halifax."

"Ah. That makes you one up on the admiral, eh?" I said archly. I was beginning to feel like my old self again, now that I knew I wasn't on the carpet. Except that I was, as I was wearing carpet slippers. "Congratulations, sir."

He regarded me crossly. "I have no interest in whatever unseemly rivalries my wife might see fit to engage in," he said. "I offered to be his host, he accepted, and that's all there is to it."

"Yes, of course, Your Honor," I said sycophantically.

Somewhat mollified, he opened his mouth to continue.

"Though," I added, "it certainly is one in the eye for Mrs. Byrd-Kustard, eh?"

"I'm not the least interested in the admiral's wife," he said sharply.

"I don't blame you. She's no Gertrude Lawrence. Still, there's no getting away from it, Your Honor, it'll be quite a feather in your cap."

"Why should I care whether it's a feather in my cap or not!" he shouted. "I don't want a feather in my cap!"

"Caps look quite good with feathers."

"Damn you, I don't even have a cap!"

"How about a feather in your Homburg?"

55

"Will you be silent! I didn't call you in here to discuss my headgear!" he shouted. "I called you in to tell you *I shall need your room!*"

Well, it was nearly as comfortable in the Shubenacadie Hotel.

The following afternoon, Friday, August 30, I delivered my speech at the Town Hall. The mayor got a bit restless when I went on, perhaps a trifle too lengthily, about my favorite subject, but the rest of it went down really well, especially the part where I praised Halifax to the skies. So I was in quite a jaunty mood again by the time I arrived back at the Lieutenant-Governor's mansion for my meeting with the P.M.

There were several others waiting in the hall to see him. The Prime Minister was giving audience in Mr. Capon's study, and streams of visitors were going in and out, as well as aides, equerries, secretaries, and the like. A single mounted policeman stood guard.

Excited servants peeked from doorways, and the hall buzzed with muted conversation. Even Mrs. Capon seemed impressed by the occasion. She saw me loitering beside the staircase and came over, her face flushed and her largish teeth glistening.

"Not that I care a damn, but this'll show her ladyship who gets the really important visitors," she said triumphantly. Then: "By the way, darlin'," she whispered, squeezing my arm, "I take back everything I said about you not being a true drinker. By God, you must have been knocking it back. When I went into your room this morning to supervise, the maid showed me your pisspot. It was filled with almost pure rum."

When I went into the study, the P.M. was complaining to his private secretary about the crush of people streaming away from the Town Hall. "Some damn fool was making a speech." He had had considerable difficulty maneuvering his bike through the crush, he said. To make matters worse, some oaf had stood on his car-buncles.

"Still," he added, "it helped to take my mind off my phlebitis, lumbago, rheumatism, and sciatica."

Cycling was Sir Robert Borden's sole eccentricity. In Ottawa, he always rode a bicycle to work on Parliament Hill.

He gave me a nod. Thus encouraged, I put in, "Bike riding doesn't seem at all a good idea, if you have all those ailments, Prime Minister."

"I need the exercise."

"Don't believe in it myself. Never stand when you can sit, and never sit when you can lie down, as Lloyd told me."

"Lloyd?"

"Lloyd George. Or was it Winston?"

"Winston?"

"Churchill."

Borden looked at me with a new respect. "Yes," he said. "Well, what is it you want?"

"Want? I don't want a thing, Prime Minister."

"Everybody who comes to my office wants something."

"You've got it all wrong, Sir Robert. I'm the intrepid birdman all the fuss is about."

"What fuss? I'm not making a fuss. Are you making a fuss, Fred?"

"This is Colonel Bandy," the private secretary explained, looking me over coldly. "He's come to pay his respects—"

"Hasn't paid many so far, has he? Bandy . . . Bandy . . . Are you that corporal that Sam Hughes promoted to assistant paymaster general? The one who immediately gave all his mates a raise?"

After these initial misunderstandings, however, I got on so well with this thick-set, modest man that the five minutes allotted to the interview stretched to nearly six.

"I sure would like him to meet Sam Hughes," Borden said, grinning at his secretary.

Hughes was Borden's former defence minister, the Orangeman from Lindsay who had done good work mobilizing the Army for war, but who had ultimately been kicked out of the government for trying to foist an inferior rifle on the infantry, and because of some scandal involving the shell-purchasing commission. "It would be quite a meeting, wouldn't it, Fred? He reminds me of Sam."

"He's a quiet, gentlemanly sort of chap, is he?" I asked.

"He's erratic, intemperate, mulish, and more than a little crazy. But I will say this for him, he knew how to stand up to the bigwigs. At the beginning of the war, when the great Lord Kitchener informed Sam that he intended splitting our Canadian divisions among the British units, Sam told him to go to hell; he had other plans for the Canadian Army. Nobody had ever talked that way to the Field Marshal before, but Sam got away with it, all right.

"Yes," he mused, "a lot of people said I should've gotten rid of Sam years ago, but I'll tell you why I didn't, Bartholomew. I needed his terrible temper. You ever flown off the handle, Bartholomew?"

"No, I don't think . . . Oh, wait. Yes, I did, once. At an English garden party."

"I've only lost mine once, in my entire political life," Borden said, removing his boots with a sigh of relief. "You know, for years I've been running myself ragged, doing everything I possibly could for the imperial war effort. Working sometimes eighteen hours a day on their behalf, and ruining my health in the process. I've give them a hell of a lot of money and material, and about half a million men, and I've just about torn this country apart in my efforts to go on supplying them with men."

"Conscription and all that."

"Yes. And you know what? For years, I never knew what was going on, except what I read in the papers. The British never told me a darned thing, Bartholomew. And when I finally confronted that Deputy Prime Minister fellow, Bonar Law, about it, you know what he told me? It wasn't convenient to keep us colonials informed, and that I had a durn cheek even suggesting they should. I should mind my own business.

"That's when I went up like the Halifax explosion. I told the government over there just what I thought of them. I said that if they'd all been German agents they couldn't have run the war more effectively—for the benefit of the enemy. I said they were a bunch of durned incompetents, and in fact I'd been secretly relieved until now not to know what was going on, so I'd be able to sleep at night; but when some arrogant expatriate Canadian like Bonar Law tells me to mind my own business, I'd had enough.

"And it got immediate results, Bartholomew. They've been buttering me up with floods of secret dispatches ever since, and keeping me meticulously informed about a great many perfidious deals I now find I'd much rather not know about. But at least they no longer treat me as if I were a quartermaster-sergeant.

"The point is, Bartholomew, all my life I've been gentlemanly and easygoing—the perfect example of Anglo-Saxon reserve, and the only time I've ever really got anywhere was when I blew up like that. That's made me realize a lot of things, Bartholomew, principally that you can talk all you like in praise of protocol, reason, and diplomacy, but it's emotion, Bartholomew, *emotion* that makes people sit up and take notice and get the lead out of their boots. So, from now on, bang, it's outburst of temper from me, whether I feel like it or not."

His private secretary leaned over and whispered in the P.M.'s hairy ear.

"Oh, yes," Borden said. "He's the one, is he?" He looked at me guardedly. "Bartholomew?"

"Yes, sir?"

"I have some interesting news for you."

"Yes, sir?"

"Your tour over here will have to be cut short."

"Oh?"

"They've got a job for you. Know anything about Russia?"

"I . . . met a Russian spy once. He sold me a samovar . . . Russia?"

"That's where you're going, Bartholomew."

"*Russia?* But it's full of socialists!"

"It's purely voluntary, of course."

"In that case, Prime Minister, I think I'll just go to Ottawa instead."

"But if you don't volunteer, I gather you're likely to end up defending the Outer Hebrides," Borden said, leaning over and regretfully drawing on his boots again. "Well, you asked for it, didn't you?"

"I didn't ask for anything," I cried indignantly. "Specially not Russia!"

"Now, now, don't lose your temper. That won't get you anywhere. What I meant was—" He stopped and looked up at his secretary. "What did I mean, Fred?"

The private secretary looked at me as if I were a common species of hornet. "You gave a final interview to the press just before you sailed from Liverpool," he said curtly. "About parachutes."

"What about it? All I said was there was a first-class parachute available that was being ignored, though it would need almost no development work whatso—"

"You said all that," the secretary interrupted, "in spite of the fact that the Air Minister had just announced that they were putting the Guardian Angel into production."

"Of course. That's *why* I said it."

"You made him look like a durn fool, Bartholomew," the Prime Minister said, a shade reprovingly. "They've been on our backs ever since."

"They're incensed about it," the secretary said. "With good reason, in my opinon."

I opened my mouth.

"Further," he said, "you went on to announce your intention of airing the subject as soon as you got back to Canada."

"And I see," Borden said, drawing a shoot of foolscap toward him and glancing at it sorrowfully, "that you did just that, Bartholomew, this afternoon."

He shook his head. "There are certain reasons why we don't wish to upset the imperial government at this time, Bartholomew," he said. "We're beginning some very delicate negotiations, you see, regarding foreign policy. It looks as if, in that regard, and in the not too distant future, that we'll be able to gain control of our own destiny."

"Yes, we're obviously ripe for independence."

"Now, now, Bartholomew, let's not be bitter. Anyway, it's not as if you haven't had a nice change, is it, getting home like this. After all, you've seen Halifax. What more can you ask?"

"I want my mummy."

The snotty secretary ignored this, perhaps because I hadn't said it loudly enough.

"Now, if you don't mind," he said, "Sir Robert's a busy man." He picked up a sheaf of bumf, paper-clipped together. "You're booked to return on the *Star of the East*, which is now loading at one of the piers opposite Upper Water Street."

"The *Star of the East?* Oh, my God."

"You're lucky," he said. "They say they'll even be able to give you back your old cabin."

Back Again

After several years of enemy submarine activity, the admiralty had finally been persuaded by one or two far-sighted, frustrated fellows in Whitehall that the enormous shipping losses might be minimized if the ships travelled in convoy.

It worked fine as far as our convoy was concerned—only five ships were sunk—but it was chaos when the survivors reached port, where too many vessels were trying to nudge into too few berths.

This was at Liverpool (known, I believe, as The Athens of the North), where over twenty of the ships had to anchor in the Mersey, ours among them.

It looked as if we'd have quite a long wait before it was our turn to hitch up to the nearest bollock. Or—bollard, was it? So I was really pleased when the first officer told me that they were sending a boat for me, to take me ashore immediately.

I thought it was because I was so important, but it turned out that they had an urgent message for me from London. Katherine was down with flu.

As the hospitals were overcrowded with war casualties and victims of the Spanish influenza, she was being nursed at home, so I didn't think she was too seriously ill. But when I spoke to her father, he said she'd been taken to the Kensington and Fulham General.

Mr. Lewis sounded so alert and clear-headed, I was frightened. "How soon can you get here, Bart?" he asked.

"There isn't a train to London for nearly three hours. Is she worse this morning, then?"

"I'm afraid she is. She had a temperature of over a hundred and five. Bart? Hello? Hello?"

"Yes?"

"Her mother's with her now. I'm just going back there.

"She keeps asking for you, Bart," Mr. Lewis said clearly.

I thought I'd be clever and get down there by air. But it took two hours to reach the nearest airdrome and talk the C.O. into giving me a ride to Croydon. By the time the aircraft actually set off, two and a half hours had elapsed. Then the plane—a D.H.9 again—had engine trouble and had to land at the R.A.F. field at Castle Bromwich.

Fortunately I knew somebody there and managed to get a lift onward, without delay, in a reliable old 504K. But it was another four hours before I got to the hospital, and by that time she was dead.

It was three days before I could really believe it, which was strange, because I was experienced; I had lost quite a few friends.

It was like being concussed. I couldn't show any grief, because I felt nothing. For that reason, I didn't want to be with her family. But there was Mr. Lewis. He had been her friend as well as her father. She had always gone to him for comfort when she was really troubled.

He smiled whenever I caught his eye, but he looked as if he were suffering some physical pain that he wanted to keep from us. I was afraid he would see through my unfeeling callousness.

I was lucky. The one and only time there was anything to hear, he heard it, and came into the spare room where I was sitting on the bed, holding her favorite cartwheel hat. He put his arm around my shoulders, and we just sat there in silence, more or less.

It was a glorious day, the day of the funeral, a beautiful September day. There was a balloon crew in an unused corner of the cemetery. They seemed to be having trouble with the winch.

The balloon was stuck at two thousand feet, its silver flanks rippling in the sun.

The padre was a full colonel. Robert Lewis, in a simple air-force tunic of the maternity type, was standing as far away from him as possible. He had taken an instant dislike to the padre. I don't know why, except that Robert tended to take a violent dislike to people before he even spoke to them. He was still staring at the padre, his eyes burning. But I don't think it was really the padre that was enraging him.

Mrs. Lewis looked old, though she held herself erect, her long, lined face turned upward defiantly. Some mourners looked at her resentfully, because she had disdained to wear the veil, traditionally used to conceal a lack of grief.

The coffin was lowered into the hole just as the balloon started to soar upward.

When she smiled, she smiled with all her heart, holding nothing back.

The last time I saw her was on the front steps of the Kensington house. The ship was leaving from some out-of-the-way pier, with no visitors allowed, and she didn't want to say good-bye in a far-off railway station, among grimy pigeons and sour smoke and chipped railway cups abandoned on gritty ledges.

To bring her up to my lips, I put one arm behind her knees and the other round her waist, and picked her up. My arms never seemed able to remember how light she was, and I very nearly heaved her over the park railings. In that civilized London way, the passers-by pretended not to notice. She had laughed, only slightly embarrassed, and kissed back enthusiastically.

That was what I remembered best about her for a long time afterwards: how extraordinarily light she was.

Mrs. Lewis was in the sitting room, gazing into the fireplace.

"Well, I'm off to the Air Ministry," I said.

"You are always off somewhere, Bartholomew," she boomed. "I hope you are not making all these journeys under the impression that travel broadens the mind. In my experience, it merely subjects one to a great many discomforts that one could suffer just as easily at home. Besides, I have never discerned any virtue in bemusing one's eyes with unfamiliar and invariably disappointing sights."

"You've travelled widely, have you, Mrs. Lewis?"

"I have. When I was a gel I once visited Marlborough. And also, I believe, Cheltenham, though naturally I would never admit to the latter. A very rowdy sort of place, as I remember."

"They want me out of the way," I said, compressing my lips in a mulish manner. "I'm an embarrassment to them."

"You are an embarrassment to everybody, Bartholomew. That is one of the things I have always liked about you. You have never given way to the self-effacement that is currently so fashionable among one's more arrogant acquaintances. Only two weeks ago I had great difficulty in distinguishing young Howard Quinzy from one of his own servants; and indeed, I only clarified the situation by holding out my umbrella half-way between them, to see who took it."

"And who did?"

"Lord Quinzy, of course. The footman only accepted hats—and cloaks, if he were in a particularly good mood."

She turned and regarded me severely. "But I am sure that you, Bartholomew, will not allow them to walk roughshod over you."

"No."

After a moment, she looked away, then said in tones I had never heard from her before, "You were good for Katherine, Bartholomew. We are most grateful for the joyous turmoil you brought to the last two years of her life."

I was surprised to see it was raining outside. The windows were swimming.

She put a hand over mine. Her hand was cold as the grate in the fireplace.

"Now she is dead. But *you* will not give way to despair."

"No."

"No—my dear Bartholomew."

The meeting this time was in the office of the new Chief of Air Staff. As well as the C.A.S. and the Minister, there were two senior advisers present, and an observer from the Foreign Office, who obviously didn't have much pull, for nobody had given him a chair.

They seemed to be settled in for a lengthy discussion, but the matter was concluded swiftly enough.

"This proposal," the Minister began, squinting irritably through the window at the cloudless sky, "to send an Air Force officer to advise the counter-revolutionary government in North Russia on how to employ the aircraft that have recently fallen into their hands—"

"Yes," I said. "I'm ready to tell them what they can do with their aircraft."

"Now look here, Bandy," the Minister said, flushing.

"I mean I'm willing, sir."

"Most people would consider it a signal honor to be selected for such a task. It demands a man of initiative, with the ability to improvise, and you've amply. . . . Damn it, man, can't you see we're doing you a favor? It's not as if we were sending you to some barbarous spot like the Persian Gulf or, or, Texas. The Russians are fairly civilized—they drink almost as much tea as we do. The fact is . . ." He was starting to run down, but the momentum of his prepared argument was such that it took up quite a bit of extra track. "The fact is, Bandy, that though we've asked you to volunteer, we could just as easily order you to go. You haven't officially been transferred to the Canadian . . . What did you say?"

"I agree, sir."

"And . . . and in spite of a few successes lately, the war is obviously . . . You agree?"

"Yes, Minister."

The Minister was now beginning to look as if he'd put his money on a thoroughbred and had just noticed that it had only three legs.

"You mean you're prepared to actually go?"

"I'm ready to leave any time, sir."

"Oh," the Minister said—doubtfully.

The Dreadful Shore

Nobody seemed to be quite sure why the Allies intervened in the civil war that followed the Russian Revolution. At least, *I* never met anyone who knew what he was doing in Russia.

The right-wingers said we were fighting for ideological reasons. (Mr. Winston Churchill, the main driving force behind intervention, hated the Communists enough to have attacked them single-handed.) The left-wingers believed that intervention was a plot, by the international financiers, to overthrow Lenin and Company because they had repudiated Russia's foreign debts. The Canadians supported the anti-Bolsheviks in the hope that this might give them a post-war trade advantage. The Czechs fought in Russia for political reasons, that the Allies might look favorably on the establishment of their new state, Czechoslovakia. The Japanese, who provided most of the manpower for the Siberian expedition, were mainly interested in getting a solid foothold on the Asian mainland and in snapping up choice pieces of China.

As for Mr. Wilson, the American President, it was his uneasiness about that same Japanese expansionism that drove him into dispatching several thousand U.S. soldiers to Siberia, following this up by sending several thousand more to Archangel, because everybody else was doing so; and then trying to pretend he wasn't intervening at all.

Initially, though, the basic motive for intervention was military.

Even at the end of August 1918, it looked as if the war would last well into the following year, and the Allied brass considered it essential that the Eastern Front should be reactivated.

It was only later that the Allies, principally Britain and France, turned their guns on the Communists for more personal reasons. It was bad enough that the Reds had failed to fight the good fight to the bitter end; the bounders had also announced their intention of overthrowing the Western democracies by world proletarian revolution. The Allies couldn't allow that sort of thing to go unchallenged. It might give their own lower classes ideas.

Though they made a considerable investment in troops and material, the Western Powers hoped to crush the Bolsheviks mainly by backing the forces that were already opposing the Red take-over.

These included the White Russians, who seemed to be doing quite well in the south, where they had recently captured Ekaterinodar, the capital of the Kuban region. However, it was the Czech Corps that had done the most effective fighting so far. Formed of men from the Slovakian part of the Austro-Hungarian Empire, the Czech Corps had fought staunchly on the Russian side throughout the war. When the Peace Treaty of Brest-Litovsk was signed by Russia and Germany, in March 1918, the Czechs had asked to be transferred to France in order to go on fighting for the Allied cause.

Their way westward, of course, was blocked by the German Army, so they had turned east, with the intention of sailing back into the fight from Vladivostok, at the Pacific end of Russia. In the process, they had been forced to battle the Bolsheviks. They had done so with such astonishing success—within weeks they had seized control of about half the Trans-Siberian Railway, a certain Captain Gaida so distinguishing himself in the process that he had been promoted to general—that the Allies decided the Czechs would be of even more use in Russia than in France, and ordered them to remain and support the Whites until the Americans and Japanese could come to their aid, through Vladivostok.

The Allies never did come to the aid of the Czechs. Most of them were so busy keeping a suspicious eye on each other, they never even got past Vladivostok.

In northern Russia, where I was sent, the action had begun as a purely military adventure, to deny the northern coastline of Russia and Finland to the German submarines. The establishment of British units at Murmansk had amply justified itself by holding down a substantial German army in Finland that might otherwise have been deployed on the Western Front.

The occupation of Archangel, however, was purely interventionist. The Royal Navy had fought its way into that port at the beginning of August, kicked out the local Bolshevik administration, and replaced it with a Provisional Northern Government under the leadership of a Mr. N. V. Chaikovsky.

Mr. Chaikovsky, I was told, had a number of aircraft at his disposal. I was to be his Air Assistant. Somehow, though, I had the feeling that the Air Minister didn't really care whom I assisted, so long as it wasn't he.

I sailed, as violently anti-Bolshevik as any red-blooded crusader in the cause of Motherhood and Profit, with a quarrelsome collection of Russians, British, French, Americans, Japanese, Serbians, Italians, and a volunteer party from the Canadian 16th Brigade, an artillery outfit. I spent most of the voyage trying to learn the rudiments of Russian.

Not since my third-year anatomy exams had I worked with such intense concentration. I sat on my bunk from morning until late at night, hunched over my grammar books, dictionary, and notebooks. A few times, when I couldn't sleep, I even got up in the middle of the night to resume my studies.

It was as good a way as any to distract myself, I suppose; and it was effective enough; I was quite distracted. By the time we reached Archangel, I had familiarized myself with the alphabet and had memorized all the numbers up to a hundred, a few common verbs, and two or three hundred nouns, and was able to repeat quite fluently such phrases as 'We wish to visit theatres, museums, and cathedrals' and 'Do you know of anyone who can mend my socks?'

The only trouble was, the Russians I shared the cabin with couldn't understand a word I said.

It was some time before I realized that the secret of that strangely constructed language, with its absence of articles and its double negatives and the like, lay in its tone. Where other civilized tongues had particles, Russian had inflection. Unless one learned to give their words the right lilt, one might just as well have conversed in Cree or Old Norse.

One of my cabin mates was an infantry general. He was very seasick indeed. He spent the first week lying on his bunk, groaning and muttering and occasionally biting a ship's biscuit in a melancholy way.

Knowing from recent experience what it was like, I did my best to make things as comfortable as possible for him, keeping him warm and bringing him cups of tea, damp cloths, and buckets. He wasn't at all grateful, though. The only time he evidenced any gratitude was when the ship yawed with more than usual violence, so that his head rolled against the ship's iron ribs with a mushy thud. He was obviously hoping to be battered unconscious, or, better still, killed outright.

I was quite surprised when I saw him standing up for the first time. Lying prone, he had looked so scrunched up and frail. Arranged more or less vertically, he turned out to be as substantial as he was hairy: he had unusually broad shoulders, and what I had taken to be an extra blanket proved to be a massive brown beard shaped like a bent spade.

I never did find out for sure what his name was. When he pronounced it, it sounded like *Brzhtvh;* but he may just have been retching.

Our other cabin mate was completely immune to the succession of storms we encountered in the North Sea. This was surprising, considering that this was his first real voyage. He had been a lifelong court official at the Imperial Palace at Tsarskoe Selo.

Count Anatole Snetkov was a man of about sixty, with a face that looked as if it had been injected with a permanent local anaesthetic. A member of the White Russian Council in Paris, he was on his way to Archangel to put the White Russian point of view to the new political regime there.

He was unlike his compatriot in every way. The general was like a bear that had just struggled out of a garbage dump, and smelled like it, too. He was pessimistic, indifferent to discomfort in the field, and violent. He had first come to our attention while we were waiting for the train to Dundee from King's Cross Station, in London. He had struck one of his soldiers for repeating Communist propaganda, knocking the man unconscious with one blow.

Though the other members of the expedition, particularly the Americans, had been outraged, nobody among the Russians appeared to find this summary discipline the least disconcerting, and I must admit it had its effect. By the time he had recovered from the concussion, the soldier was quite converted to the ways of democracy.

By contrast, the count was slender, dapper, and stilted in his relations with ordinary people. He dressed fastidiously and was a devil for perfume. As soon as he'd finished dressing in the morning, he took out a cut-glass scent spray from his inlaid toilet case and sprayed himself practically all over, until he smelled like an acre of sodden lilacs.

For the first few days, the count made no effort to converse, beyond the stiff apologies our close confinement made necessary. One evening, however, he returned from one of his marathon bridge games in the brown Windsor wardroom that served as a salon on that drab ship, to find me trying to sew on the expedition shoulder patch, a white star on a blue background. After watching me for several minutes with mounting impatience, he snatched the needle and thread and sewed the patch on for me, neatly and quickly.

"Thank you very much. That's very nice."

A smirk wrenched desperately at his frozen features. "The Grand Duchess Tatiana Nicolayevna herself taught me to sew," he said, biting off the thread and handing back my tunic between thumb and forefinger, as if passing over an angry cat.

After a moment, he went on stiffly, "I see you are an aviator, *Monsieur*. You are to fly in Russia, then?"

"I'm to be air assistant to your Mr. Nicholas V. Chaikovsky."

"Nicholas V. Chaikovsky . . . ?"

"Governor of the Archangel Administration."

"Oh, yes? Dear me, I cannot keep up with all these new people who are springing up like weeds."

"Isn't he the man you're supposed to advise, Count?"

"Perhaps," Snetkov said vaguely, and, changing the subject, went on to complain about the British. It seemed they had been unable to make room for the count's personal servants.

"That's too bad."

"I told them I had not been without servants for fifty years. They continued to refuse, even though I offered to keep my servants *en arrimage*."

"In storage? With labels on them, Count? 'Not Wanted on Voyage,' that sort of thing?"

"Of course not," he said, looking at me with a frown. "What an absurd notion, my dear Colonel." He flapped his wrist and sniffed. "They would have been safe enough in the hold *without* labels."

Over the next day or two, he told me quite a bit about his life in the Alexander Palace, near Petrograd (or St. Petersburg, as he still called it). It appeared that he had spent almost his entire life in the imperial palace.

He gave the impression that his duties had been onerous but stimulating. I noticed, though, that he was careful to avoid defining what his position was. I began to suspect that he hadn't had an official title, but was just one of the vast number of courtiers whose energies had been applied exclusively to the service of the Tsar and his family.

This impression was confirmed one morning when, perhaps not properly awake and on guard, he let slip the information that it had been his job to arrange the royal correspondence.

"You mean, that's all you did?" I asked. "Sort the mail?"

He looked at me like an offended catfish, and wouldn't speak to me for the rest of the day.

I learned later, though, from a former royal official in Archangel (*his* job had been to summon the yamshchik, or imperial troika-driver), that I hadn't been far wrong. Snetkov wasn't high enough in the hothouse hierarchy even to *open* the correspondence. All he did was shuffle it into neat piles—letters from relatives, invitations, threatening notes from anarchists, ads for corsets and the like, and dump all the invoices in the jewelled Fabergé waste bin.

He was so annoyed with me he spent the next two days on the lookout for ways to put me in my place. The following evening, for instance, when I used the word *Tsar*, he replied witheringly, "What is this *Tsar* and *Tsarina* you are always talking about? My dear Colonel, except to historians, the words are entirely unknown in Russia. These titles are the products of ignorant journalists. One never hears them in Russia."

"Oh."

"His Majesty the Emperor Nicholas is referred to as *Godusar Imperator*, never as *Tsar*. Similarly, Her Royal Highness is *Imperatritza*. And that poor boy of theirs is not *Tsarevitch* but *Nadslyednik*. *Tsarevitch* indeed!"

"Thank you, Count. By the way, what exactly is wrong with the *Nadslyednik?* Is it true he has haemophilia?"

"Nads*lyed*nik," he said, wearily correcting my pronunciation. Then, dismissively: "You will forgive me, Colonel, but we do not discuss the state of health of His Royal Highness outside the royal circle."

It seemed to me that, for a government adviser, he was slightly out of touch. He talked as if the imperial court were still in existence. When I asked where the Royal Family was now (their whereabouts were still unknown, though there were rumors that they were incarcerated, under harsh conditions, in Siberia), he looked at me as if to say, My good man, where else would they be but making their rounds of the palaces at Tsarskoe Selo, exercising their dogs, and sacking their ministers.

He didn't actually say the Royal Family was still reigning at Tsarskoe Selo, for then he would have had to explain to himself what he'd been doing in exile, as a member of the White Russian Council; but his whole attitude seemed to deny all that had happened in Russia since March 1917.

However, if he wanted to live in the past it was all right with me. Maybe he was a lot better off back there.

All the same, when he went on to talk as if the whole of Russia were still in raptures of affection for the Royal Family, I couldn't help murmuring that events seemed to suggest the opposite.

"That is nonsense," he said sharply. "The Russian peoples love their Little Father." There was not a time when His Royal Highness went out, to hunt, for instance, that his entourage did not return with breathless accounts of the almost mystic adoration in which he was held. "You are a foreigner, of course, my dear, so you cannot understand the almost religious devotion to the Royal Family that permeates the soul of the Russian people. Once, His Royal Highness was approaching a village that was in danger of being washed away during the unusually wet autumn of 1911. The *Imperator,* of course, had braved the elements regardless, refusing to alter his schedule merely because of a temporary inclemency in the weather—conditions that would have sent any ordinary man scuttling for shelter— Ah, what courage he has! Alors, just as he was riding along the hill overlooking the flooded village—the rain stopped. The rain stopped—just like that! The very moment he appeared! As they floated past on their houses, the peasants realized it was a miracle, and would undoubtedly have prostrated themselves before their Little Father, had the configurations of their roofs permitted it."

By then, Brzhtvh had started to recover. He was sitting up on his bunk, listening wanly to the count's babblings. I waited expectantly, for I knew that the general was exceedingly hostile to Nicholas II and Alexandra.

He had told me so only a couple of nights before, while I was tucking him up after a particularly severe bout of vomiting. "At one time, Bandyeh, I would have given my life for the Emperor," he croaked. He brought a couple of huge hands from beneath the blankets and held them up shakily. "I personally, Bandyeh, personally strangled the first man in my regiment to raise the red flag. With these very hands I throttled that man until his eyes fell onto his cheeks." His hands fell limply onto the bed. "But now, though I will kill every one of those Soviet swine if given the opportunity"—his face flushed as rage stirred up his blood—"I realize that all our troubles have come from the Emperor and that German bitch of his, with her priests and lickspittles. If I met them today, I would spit at their feet."

So I expected him at any moment to start pounding the count's anaesthetized face in the berserk fury he was noted for, crying, "If everybody loved the Emperor so much, then how, you cut-glass ornament, do you account for the revolution?!"

But all Brzhtvh did was to listen somewhat inattentively and nod, and occasionally smile vaguely through the undergrowth.

I couldn't understand Brzhtvh's indifference, unless he was even more demoralized than he looked. As soon as the count had left, I said as provocatively as my mood would allow, "The count talks a lot of sense, don't you think?"

"Ha?"

"About the Tsar."

Brzhtvh shrugged, looking at me with a queer, speculative sort of look. "He's strange fellow," he said in English. "He reminds me of schoolteacher, when I was in kindergarten . . . Used to tell us wery good stories when he wasn't hitting us."

"What kind of stories?"

"Fairy tales, I suppose . . ."

"Ah."

He was still looking at me in that strange way. He said suddenly, "You like me, eh, Bandyeh?"

"H'm?"

"You have fancy for me?"

"Eh?"

"A fancy for me?"

I gazed back at him, equally interrogatively. "Fancy? How do you mean, sir?"

"You have been good to me, Bandyeh. Bringing tea. Mopping the brow. Cleaning up the sick. Tucking me into bonk. Come, I understand."

He lifted the corner of his blanket a trifle resignedly, as if he wasn't really in the mood for exposing his grubby sheets but felt that he should reciprocate for all I'd done for him.

Except—why should he think I was interested in his grubby sheets?

"You have been wery tender, Bandyeh."

That word tender made me feel kind of uncomfortable. It seemed rather a soppy word for him to use. "Oh, I wouldn't say that," I mumbled.

"So? Now I am better, Bandyeh. We are alone, yes?"

"Eh?"

Brzhtvh smiled. A tooth glinted through his brown beard.

"I'm sorry, I don't know what you're talking about, General."

His tooth winked. "You are wery delicate, Bandyeh. I like that. You are nice man."

To my annoyance, I felt myself flushing. Well, it was those mushy words, and that sort of mushy look on his face. I much preferred his usual lethal expression. Also, I don't know why, but the drift of the conversation was making me decidedly uneasy.

"Don't know what you're on about," I muttered, kicking the count's luggage. "Much rather you didn't talk like that, General. Humph. Think I'll go up and get some fresh air."

When I looked at him again, he was staring.

"But—"

"See you later."

"Wait. Bandyeh? You mean—you do not have fancy?"

I drew myself up—as far as the deck overhead would allow—and said a bit coldly, "Your English is quite good, General, but there are certain words that really should be avoided when talking to a chap.

Tender, and . . . *nice,* and dreadful words like that. You're not really supposed to use them, you know. At least not to another fellow, you know."

Having set the record straight. I went out, leaving him, for some reason, a bit open-mouthed.

When I got back, he was still looking pallidly puzzled. However, I assumed this was because he was having to listen to the count again.

Snetkov had also returned, and already had his manicure equipment spread all over the place and was filing and polishing his nails and talking to Brzhtvh in French about the time he had accompanied the *Imperatritza* on a visit to a Red Cross hospital at Pskov.

Snetkov remembered the occasion well, he said, because it was only the second time in his life that he had been away from Tsarskoe Selo. He was enthusing almost girlishly. "Ah, my General," he was trilling, "if you could have seen the expressions on the faces of the common soldiers when their Little Mother appeared by their bedside in that hospital. They looked up at her with such anxiety that one could not help but be moved almost to tears, almost to tears. Moreover, Her Majesty was in a simple nurse's uniform. Just imagine it, she had come as an ordinary nurse!"

"What happens then?" Brzhtvh asked with a simple smile.

"Alors, as she questioned the soldiers—in her astonishingly good Russian as, strangely enough, none of the soldiers spoke French— their anxiety gave way to looks of the most touching perplexity— almost as if they couldn't understand a word she was saying."

He emitted a little giggle, and flapped his wrists in a way that deepened my suspicions of him still further. "Though of course they were merely torn between bedazzlement at the Presence and humbled by the awareness of their own insignificance." He glanced at me coquettishly. "The Russians, you see, Colonel, have a profound religious sense of humility. One of the soldiers was so affected that he tried to struggle up, his face contorted in an expression of almost frightening humility. He tried to answer her, though it must have cost him an effort, for his teeth were clenched. A less perceptive man than I could quite easily have mistaken his passion of loyalty for one of incoherent rage and hatred. Even Her Imperial Majesty could not help looking slightly uneasy.

"Unfortunately, on that same occasion, the imperial visit was marred by the scandalous behavior of one of the hospital doctors—a selfish request that the *Imperatritza* might wish to appear at a parade of the local School of Cadets, so that the young lads might be inspired by a glimpse of their Empress before their departure for the front. But of course her itinerary could not possibly be altered." The count's lips tightened. "In spite of which, the doctor had the effrontery to allow the boys to line up along her route, behind a railway fence. The Empress would have been entirely justified in ignoring them completely; and in fact had a perfect excuse for doing so, as little could be seen of the boys behind the fence boards apart from pairs of wide-open eyes and the occasional nose. Nevertheless she nodded at the fence most graciously as she sped by."

Over the previous few days, I'd had a growing suspicion about the count. It increased still further as he flapped his hands about, to dry his nail varnish. I was certain that he was one of those people I'd heard about who were not entirely, well, sexually normal. *You* know.

To confirm my suspicions, I asked casually, as I leaned against his trunk—his luggage, I mean—I wouldn't have come anywhere near his actual trunk—"By the way, Count—you're not married, I suppose?"

"Pardon?" He seemed to be having difficulty adjusting to this change of subject. "But yes . . . ?"

"You *are?*"

"Certainly. Why do you ask that, dear?"

"Oh . . . just, just wondered," I said.

But perhaps his marriage was a cover for his sordid leanings. "Got any children?" I asked subtly.

"As I said before, *Monsieur*, you make some very strange remarks . . . I have eight children."

"You do?"

"Certainly. Olga, Vera, Petya, Nina, Maria, Elizaveta, Sonya, and Gladys."

"*Gladys?*"

"Such a beautiful English name, don't you think?"

"I . . . yeah," I said, wondering how I could have been so wrong. He was obviously as normal as Brzhtvh.

On the second-last day of the voyage, a wireless message for the general was delivered to the cabin. After ten hours of Russian studies, I needed some fresh air and offered to deliver it to him.

I found him at the stern of the ship with his batman. They were huddled closely together behind a life raft, with their arms around each other.

Brzhtvh seemed an unusually democratic sort of chap, I thought.

As Brzhtvh read the signal, the batman, pale and shrunken inside his British khaki, leered and vanished into the gloom.

"I knew that already," Brzhtvh muttered, and tossed the signal into the White Sea, which of course was grey. "I am to join Slavo-British Legion in Archangelsk."

"M'm."

"If they have not already deserted to Reds."

"Ah."

"Still, as we Russians say, *If a man has many kopecks in his pocket, he jingles as he walks.*"

I gazed dully across at the dreadful coastline of northern Russia.

"*Tyem nyeh myenyeh, na Moskvu.*"

"I hope so," I muttered. "I don't like the look of this place at all."

The White Sea coast was as leaden as the dusk. No houses, no sign of cultivation, just miles and miles of melodramatic forest.

"Don't go, Colonel. Talk."

"What about?"

"I am puzz-led, Bandyeh. I have asked about you. I have learned that you are great hero of British Air Force. You have more than fifty air victories, yes?"

"M'm."

"You were also fine infantry officer. They say you should have received Wictoria Cross."

I shifted uncomfortably.

"But you are so unhappy, Bandyeh."

"No, no."

"Is because you are going to Russia?"

"I volunteered."

"How do you feel about Bolsheviks?"

"Viciously."

"Is not good to be unhappy alone, Bandyeh."

A chill, damp breeze flapped his long, grey greatcoat, and riffled his whiskers.

"You think I am too coarse to understand, Bandyeh?"

"No, no."

"You think I am great, hairy, disgusting Russian."

"Why on earth should I think that?"

"Prove you do not disapprove of me. Confide, Bandyeh. Confide."

I had no alternative, unless I were to seem cold and hostile. I told him much more than I'd intended, and when I'd finished he put an arm around me and wept, to keep me company.

It was my first experience of that aspect of the Russian soul: that wholehearted willingness to lessen the anguish of others by sharing in it.

"I love you, Bandyeh. But in good way, you understand."

I turned away, to wipe my face.

"Come, Bandyeh. Let us end it all in the cabin."

I thought he was proposing a suicide pact. But he was only referring to the whisky.

We reached Archangel on September 24. I had orders to report first to the Allied commander, General Poole, but when I finally managed to ease a way through the importunate throng of merchants, refugees, civil servants, and high Russian officers at Army H.Q., the harried British major who seemed to be dealing with the mob single-handed said it wasn't much use consulting Poole, because he had been replaced. General Ironside was taking over as Commander-in-Chief of the Allied and White Russian Forces. He wasn't due in Archangel for several days. However, the major would make a note of my name, and in the meantime I should just carry on to my unit, next please.

"I'm not with any unit. I'm attached to Chaikovsky."

"Yes, sir, and I'm quite fond of Chopin, but I don't quite see what that has to do with it."

"Mr. Nicholas V. Chaikovsky, the chief of the new government."

"What new government?"

"The new White Russian Government. Up here in Archangel."

"Oh, them. They were thrown out last week."

"Thrown out?"

"Another *coup d'état*, I suppose."

"What's happened to Chaikovsky, then?"

"Shot, I imagine. He was a socialist, you see."

As it happened, Chaikovsky hadn't been shot but had suffered an even worse fate: he had been made President.

As such, he had even less power than when he was Governor. A British First Secretary told me so, and advised me to seek fresh instructions from the Air Ministry, which I did very promptly after meeting Mr. Chaikovsky.

He was seventy years old, with a yellow-and-white beard, and spent most of his time in pointless administrative wrangling and in issuing proclamations that nobody read, because everyone knew it was the British who were running the show.

Naturally he hadn't been told I was coming, and knew nothing about me. He began to look interested, though, when I brought up the subject of aircraft, and he was half-way through a declaration of White Russian air policy before he discovered that I wasn't offering him aircraft but asking where *his* were.

"I'm supposed to advise you on the best use of your equipment, sir."

"*Mon cher,*" he quavered, "there appears to have been some slight misunderstand. We have no airplanes at all. You are quite sure you have no *escadrilles* to offer us? No matter; we have no need for such frivolities. A few regiments of our splendid White Russian soldiers are all we shall need against the dastardly Bolsheviks, who are quite plainly on the point of collapse."

As he rose to signify that the audience was at an end, there was a faint phut, and another bullet hole appeared in the window behind him. "It's nothing," he said, watching me in amused disdain as I crouched behind his desk. "Just one of our dear boys in the barracks across the street, having his little amusement."

As nobody would admit responsibility for me, I had some difficulty in obtaining official accommodation. Brzhtvh solved the problem by getting me a room in a requisitioned house occupied by White Russian officers. It was next door to the technical school that served as American Army headquarters.

The other occupants were high officers of the Russian Army, all of them wearing prodigious numbers of medals that rang like field telephones whenever they took more than two steps (usually toward the bar). They accepted my foreign presence with admirable complaisance. As for me, I was happy to be in their company, partly because I was becoming very fond of Russians, but mostly because it afforded me an opportunity to continue practicing my Russian on people who were too well-bred to cringe at my pronunciation.

Days later, I was still in Archangel, waiting for fresh instructions to come through from London. In the meantime, between baffling conversations with the senior officers, some of whom had taken to sneaking back to their rooms as soon as they heard me pronounce the words *dobroye ootro,* I went sightseeing.

Archangel was, in normal times, a city of forty-eight thousand souls, clinging narrowly to the shore at the mouth of the Dvina River. I was drably surprised by its appearance. I'd visualized something like a Canadian arctic settlement with a few Russian touches: droshkies, samovars, Cossacks in tcherkasses, *alfresco* church services with deep-voiced choirs, and people getting excited about metaphysics as they knouted their serfs, with others lying around on stoves complaining about life. Well, they always seemed to be doing that sort of thing in Russian novels.

But if you'd seen them scuttling along Sparks or Wellington Street in winter, you couldn't have distinguished the Archangel citizen from the Ottawa resident. The city was similarly full of contrasts, a queer mixture of substantial villas and frame or log hovels, of minarets and the blackened chimneys of jobless mills. There were sophisticated buildings as massive and ugly as you'd find in any civilized spot. Right next to them, open sewers with an almost visible miasma.

Dominating the city, and indeed the whole countryside, was a splendid cathedral with a blue-and-gold cupola and four graceful spires. Not many paces away, the Café de Paris, where the whores teemed.

The main street of the city was the Troitsky Prospekt. Curving around the bay, parallel to the shoreline, it was macadamized for most of its length; a busy, bustling thoroughfare, loud with wheeled and pedestrian traffic, trolley cars flashing and swaying, gaudily attired officers and a few well-dressed ladies strolling and gossiping and haughtily acknowledging salutes under the electric lamps with their misty halos.

A few yards behind this sophisticated thoroughfare were streets so wet and muddy that even the stepping stones were hard put to it to keep their heads above water.

The old Russian tricolour hung limply in the muggy air from every flagpole in the city—except in the industrial suburb of Solombala, at the northern end. There were no flags visible there, though judging by the hostile attitude of the factory workers, I had an idea they had plenty of red flags tucked away for future use.

The crowds were just as varied as the city: refugee peasants from outlying towns, many of them pinched and penniless, humbly stepping off the wooden sidewalks for the local toffs; plump, well-to-do merchants and their families from as far away as Petrograd, hoping for passages on Allied ships before the White Sea froze over and the Red Menace engulfed the peninsula; dock-workers with sullen, downcast eyes; worried, discontented diplomats—the foreign diplomatic corps had recently moved here from Petrograd; and thousands of Russian, British, French, and American soldiers and sailors who were just as strongly contrasted as the setting: the Russians bewildered and disheveled, the British war-weary, the French cynical, the Americans bright-eyed and interested (except when they looked at the native girls, who were all uncommonly dumpy, with large behinds and no waists).

Sightseeing soon palled, however, and gradually I found myself doing what all the other officers did: I paced up and down the Troitsky Prospekt, stopping here for a coffee and there for a vodka. I certainly had lots of aimless company. There were hundreds of unemployed Russian officers in the city, and they and the wealthy citizens and senior government employees seemed to be having a frenziedly good time in Archangel, dancing, gorging, gossiping, crowding the cafés in loud-laughing parties, staggering away from all-night drinking sessions, joshing and preening. After three days, I was desperate to get away from the place.

My hopes soared when I met a British 2nd-lieutenant pilot and his observer, and learned that they were on their way to an airfield that had been established at a place called Obozerskaya.

I knew the Navy was operating seaplanes in the area, but it was the first time I'd heard that the R.A.F. was also in northern Russia.

"What are you flying?" I asked eagerly.

"Strutters."

"Sopwith Strutters? Oh. Still—is there any room for another pilot?"

"I shouldn't think so," the pilot said, looking at me curiously. "They already have too many."

There were only five aircraft at Obozerskaya, he said. They were machines that had been found at Murmansk, still crated, though they had been delivered to the imperial Russian forces nearly two years before.

The Russians had never got around to unpacking them.

Unfortunately, there were about twenty Russian and British flyers competing for these five aircraft. Obviously the C.O. wasn't going to welcome yet another pilot, especially a thoroughly shop-soiled colonel with a face like a despairing camel.

That same afternoon, I encountered General Brzhtvh again, just as he was coming out of Army H.Q. He had been upriver at Khol-mogori for the past few days.

He was in one of his elated moods, and greeted me with a spectacular embrace right there on the street, as if I'd been in the Château d'If for twenty years. Seizing my arm, he hurled me into the nearest café.

With one look, he swept a table clear of five sky-blue cavalry officers.

"Vodka!" he shouted jovially, smashing the table with his fist. As a waiter scuttled up with a bottle and glasses: "And tell me, Band-yeh, what you have been doing."

I told him, in a frightful mixture of Russian and French. He listened, gripping his beard between his thumb and finger. He was always trying to straighten it in this fashion, but it continued to remain bent.

"Good," he said. "Good!" He banged the table again. "You would be wasting your time with these lapdogs. As we say in Russia, *Only a foolish crane flies north in the winter.*"

He drilled me with his fierce, fierce eyes. "Tell me, Bandyeh. Would you be interested in joining Slavo-British Legion?"

I stared back at him. *"Eta mozhna?"*

"Da!"

"The Air Ministry said I was now to consider myself under General Poole's orders. Can you arrange it with him?"

"General Poole agrees to everything I say. He does not care, he is leaving in few days."

Before I had a chance to change my mind, I said in my very best Russian, *"Ya k vashim oosloogam."*

"Eh?"

"I am at," I said, "your service."

Disguised
as a Bear

The training base for the White Russian Army was forty-two miles up the Dvina River from Archangel, at Kholmogori. It was a seaport threatened by grey forest and muskeg, with clouds to match.

Even the numerous tall churches seemed to have difficulty holding up the leaden sky. Somebody told me that the golden onion domes and spires were gilded that way in order to provide the town with a spot of celestial street-lighting. At this latitude, the sun was barely able to heave itself above the horizon in winter, and the domes and spires were supposed to help illuminate the town during the four or five hours of winter daylight, by catching and reflecting stray helpings of vitamin D.

If that was the idea, it was a sheer waste of gold paint. All the time I was there, the sun shunned northern Russia as if it had orders not to relieve the monochrome with even the most watery of beams.

The centre of town, with its churches, military establishments, and administrative buildings, was in fairly good shape, but it seemed to me there was a certain indefinable air of neglect about the dock area: toppled cranes, collapsed warehouses, crumbled quays, piers buckling at the knees, and sunken barges protruding slimily from the silted harbor.

"As a seaport," I remarked to my adjutant, Major Poupychev, "Kholmogori would seem to leave something to be desired."

"Has not been used as seaport for two hundred years."

"Oh."

"Not since Archangelsk became deep-sea port for northern Russia."

"I thought it was just a bit run down, like everything else in Russia."

Major Poupychev looked at me in rather an offended way. He was a ponderous, pessimistic man of about forty-five, with bright, wet lips set in a plump, heavy face. He looked as if he had just been sucking red lollypops, or chewing betel nuts. His lips glistened like crimson slugs. Rather amorous slugs, when he compressed them, as he was doing now.

Though not too prepossessing, Poupychev was a reasonably good administrator, when forced to rouse himself from his lethargy.

"Your orders, Bartalamyeh Fyodorevitch?" he asked stiffly. (My father's Christian name was Frederick, so they called me Bartholomew Fyodorevitch—Bartholomew, son of Frederick.)

"Same as today. Exercises by company and platoon. We must get the men used to moving fast across country. And at the risk of being tedious, I must also say it is important that they learn not to throw away their equipment when it becomes too heavy, Vladimir Petrovitch."

"It is impossible to move fast at this time of year, Colonel. There is too much mud." He looked at my boots. "As you have already found." His own boots were brilliantly polished.

"We must try nevertheless, Vladimir Petrovitch," I said with an encouraging scowl.

Since the beginning of October, I'd been in charge of four decidedly under-strength companies of White Russian troops, spending most of the day slogging about with the men on training exercises, and most of the night reading old infantry training manuals to find out what I'd been doing during the day.

Though they were supposed to be half-way through their advanced training, half the men still didn't even know how to aim their long Russian rifles properly, let alone grasp the idea of military discipline as a means of getting individuals to act in concert. They skylarked about at target practice, pricked each other for fun

84

at bayonet practice, fell asleep during lectures, and marched like girl guides with chapped thighs.

Taking into consideration the time we had at our disposal and the kind of terrain we would have to traverse, I had decided to eliminate any kind of physical training or drill, or technical instruction except of the most rudimentary kind, and to concentrate on encouraging them to aim their rifles instead of just shooting them off a hundred feet above the target, and in teaching them only the most basic tactical lessons: how to establish advance, flank, and rear guards, how to circle around enemy positions, how to co-ordinate their attacks, how to give each other covering fire, and how to take up defensive positions once they'd attained their objective.

Everything else in the book I threw out, from saluting to march discipline, and all the hundred other details a knowledge of which helped to compose the well-made infantryman. Apart from anything else, there was no time for more. General Brzhtvh had ordered his regiment to be ready to join in the attack on Emtsa and Plesetskaya about the middle of October.

Emtsa and Plesetskaya were respectively 100 and 120 miles south of Archangel on the Archangel-to-Vologda railway. At Vologda, this railway intersected the Trans-Siberian Railway, and there was the entire explanation for the Allied strategy: to get astride the Trans-Siberian at Vologda and use it to link up with the Czechs and White Russians in Siberia. This accomplished, and with General Denikin pressing up from the south toward Moscow, the Bolshevik Government would be completely encircled, and would stand little chance of surviving.

The men didn't seem to mind my crude efforts, but the officers were pretty upset about it. Though there were a handful of British officers in other Slavo-British units, in mine they were all Russians, and they remonstrated haughtily against the abandonment of all conventional discipline, especially saluting. The ex-Tsarists particularly enjoyed being saluted. They had been brought up in the old tradition, and still seemed to think that saluting was their main responsibility; though occasionally, if their mornings were clear of hang-overs, they were prepared to make brief appearances on parade, to get the latest gossip from the sergeants.

Major Poupychev personified the strange attitude to life that seemed to smother the soul of officer, soldier, and civilian alike. He expected nothing of the future but misfortune and calamity. There wasn't a single ounce of hope in his bulky frame.

"It's no use trying, Colonel. It is impossible to make our Russian Army efficient."

"Why not?"

"We are too badly organized."

Like the others, he saw no point in even trying to shield himself from fate. "Take our last commander, our much revered Pavel Pavlevitch. He tried for *days* to get the men to march in step, but always they would end up in convulsions, like caterpillars with many sore feet. Finally he went back to bed, and was run over by a vehicle."

"In bed?"

"He made the mistake of getting up again, you see. He went to visit his lady friend in Archangelsk. On the way, he was run over by a droshky. On purpose, we heard, by one of those Bolshevik curs from Solombala. We thought of investigating the incident, but . . . However, we did complain very bitterly to the British about it."

The officers were capable of sudden bursts of sublime enthusiasm, and would work energetically for several hours, or sometimes even for a day or two, with joyous expressions; but as these moods were invariably succeeded by deeper passivity than before, I came to dread their energy almost as much as their inertia. I had difficulty enough coping with my own depression.

Not that *they* suffered in silence, sensible fellows. The mess was usually loud with vitriolic criticism of other people, inspired self-disparagement, and violent analyses of the world's ills (for which, of course, they saw no cure). How they could spout, those handsome, elegant, beautifully mannered officers, with bitter eloquence and cynical, theatrical laughter; continually contradicting themselves, but always ready with an illogical but brilliantly argued justification of their own contrariness. I quite enjoyed these tirades, until it occurred to me that if they put their rationalized inaction into action, I would be the one to get the blame.

"All the same," I said one day in the mess, during a discussion on the virtues of being an intelligent cabbage, "even if one's destiny is unavoidable—and I don't believe that for a moment—it would be much more exhilarating to try to circumvent one's fate, rather than just do nothing."

They all looked quite intrigued at this novel thought, and to give them their due they considered it quite carefully before dismissing it as an example of the strange ways of thinking of the Mysterious West.

"No, my dear Bartalamyeh Fyodorevitch," elegant, drawling Lieutenant Togonidze summed up, "there is nothing to touch the intellectual satisfaction in rationalizing one's inertia, or the sheer emotional joy of having one's worst forebodings come true. As we Russians say, *He who drinks from a horse trough must also eat oats.*"

(I was always being brought up sharp by these Russian proverbs of theirs. *Only a hungry wolf will eat a lawyer. A cottage built from old wood is an old cottage. Many a snowflake lands on the coat of a fat woman. Even a rabbit can bite the ear of a sleeping bear.* By the time I'd worked out the relevance of their proverbs, I'd forgotten what the subject was that they were supposed to be illustrating.)

As it turned out, though, while details irked them, and while they were congenitally incapable of understanding the needs of their men, the officers proved themselves more than ready to fling themselves into battle—preferably armed with something dramatic and useless, such as a cavalry sword. They were all brave men when faced with death. If they had had half as much fortitude in the face of life, they would have been invincible.

"The snow feels colder to the peasant whose thatch is afire," as Lieutenant Bodrov summed it up.

Though I grew very fond of them, officers and men, I found their fatalistic attitude extremely annoying; until one day it occurred to me that perhaps the difficulty lay in my attitude, not theirs.

One Sunday, I attended one of their Russian Orthodox Church services.

Actually it all seemed extremely unorthodox to me—quite unsettling and totally unfamiliar. There was no pulpit in the church, nowhere to sit and fidget, not even an organ. Furthermore, it was so dark that five minutes elapsed before I realized I was standing behind a pillar.

Things weren't much clearer after I'd shuffled into the open. There were hundreds upon hundreds of people in the great cavern of the church, but they could be felt (and smelled) rather than seen. It was only gradually that I felt my senses brushed by impressions of almost uncivilized opulence: the gold and silver and ornate brass gleaming faintly in shivery patterns, illuminated by thousands of candles; precious stones, winking like stars, set in barbaric, breath-taking icons; marble columns soaring into a darkness so profound that it seemed, up there, like the day of creation minus one.

It was when the choir boomed into that startling harmony of theirs that I began to understand. The hymn was so dramatic, so strange, so orchestral, the boys sounding like violas, the men like double basses, so totally, completely beyond one's experience—it was then I began to realize that I had been thinking of the Russians as rather odd Europeans, living on the eastern extremities of Western Civilization. But—was it not more likely that, far from being the most easterly of Westerners, they were, in fact, the most westerly of Easterners?

By Jove, I thought—they're really Orientals!

From then on, their fatalism and blind acceptance of destiny began to make sense. And I was more or less able to cope with it, not by argument or reason, but by convincing them that, in all my impulsiveness and lack of logic, I was their destiny.

This made them gloomier than ever.

After several twelve-hour days of field exercises by sections and platoons, we set aside a day for three companies—the fourth was a shrunken headquarters company—to play the roles of attacker and defender in one large exercise.

The result was awful. Two platoons of attackers got lost in the woods, one platoon misread its compass and went downriver instead of up, and the remainder got so excited by the colorful display of furious Very lights, they forgot that the purpose of the fireworks display was to co-ordinate their attacks. When they finally shambled forward to the attack, they did so piecemeal and at five-to-ten-minute intervals. In battle, they would have been leisurely wiped out.

As for the defenders under the command of Captain Kisselev, they dug in along the river efficiently enough, but after several hours of rain and discomfort, half of them sneaked back to their barrack stoves. The ones who remained, crowned the shambles by standing up for a better view, as soon as the attackers started ambling forward (in, of course, small, good-natured parties).

Tiny little Captain Kisselev was very annoyed. I had some difficulty in getting him to put away his Nagent revolver. He had threatened to shoot several of the temporary deserters personally.

He finally saw reason. "Then I shall have them flogged," he compromised.

I persuaded him just to give his men a good talking-to. I had an idea that would do the trick, as Kisselev had considerable force of personality, in spite of his stature. He was so short I could look straight down into his dandruff. He was barely four feet eleven in his knee-high boots.

He was also extraordinarily good-looking, a miniature Lothario, and equally 'haughty, gallant and gay.' His splendid black eyes were shielded by the longest eyelashes I'd ever seen on either a man or a woman, and they were so spiky that when he lowered them it looked as if he had black lines painted below his eyes. These features, along with his tiny but perfectly proportioned figure, must have roused his women friends into a perfect frenzy of maternal lust. He looked more like a doll than an infantryman.

He was also the most ruthless and efficient man in the battalion, perhaps because his mother had been German. A baroness, somebody said. Prussian.

I tried to set him an example the next morning when I packed all three hundred men into the largest barracks room available. As my interpreter, a civilian appointed by the Archangel administration, had gone absent without leave (we never saw him again), I was forced to address the men in Russian. After weeks of constant and devoted practice, my grammar and accent were now merely contemptible.

"Men," I croaked, "you did fine, just fine."

I was still hoarse from shouting and groaning the whole of the previous day, and still damp from the downpour and from wading through various swamps. "However," I went on, "I'm sure you will agree we've all learned a few lessons from yesterday's exercise. Can anyone suggest how things might have been improved?

"Anyone? Speak up, lads. Is there anything we didn't do that we should have done, or anything we did do that should have been done differently. Anyone?"

They just sat there like steamed puddings. I tried several times to get a response—*any* response—but they all seemed to think it had all gone off quite splendidly.

"For instance, the attackers: do any of you think that it might have been better if you'd kept your blank cartridges until it was time to use them during the exercise, instead of shooting them off at each other as soon as they were issued?"

No answer was the stern reply. They just shuffled and snickered, picked their noses and nudged each other. A couple of the officers, who didn't like the proletarian odor, tried to sneak out.

I was on the point of giving up when I caught the eye of one of the headquarters runners, Ufan. He was a thin, ungainly fellow with such wide gaps between his teeth that he looked like an unkempt tower, with battlements. The day before, while waiting in vain for position reports at battalion H.Q. (a ditch at the edge of a pine forest), I had overheard a rib-nudging exchange between a couple of the men that seemed to indicate that Ufan had spent more than one night on the stove with a local lass named Vera Petrovna. I wondered if Vera's home was one destination that Ufan *had* managed to locate.

In desperation I said, "What about Ufan there, lads. Does anyone think the day might have gone even more successfully if he had delivered his messages *before* he went off to visit Vera Petrovna?"

For a moment, I thought I'd got it all wrong and was making a dreadful fool of myself. Then somebody tittered, and when I affixed a wry smile, a shout of laughter went up. Some of Ufan's pals started pounding him on the back. Ufan smirked sheepishly, and shuffled, showing his gap teeth, which further increased the merriment.

After that, seeing I wasn't in an accusing mood, the suggestions started to come in; haltingly at first, then in a rush. Most of them were useless—one chap suggested that next time we should pick a fine day instead of a rainy one—but there was enough self-criticism left over to make it unnecessary for me to underline more than one or two of the most important points.

As a result, morale soared from the depths of melancholy to the heights of pessimism, a great improvement; and, among others, Ufan took to saluting me every time we met, thinking it would please me.

I told him and a cluster of others that if the Bolsheviks could get along without saluting, so could we. It was much more important for them to learn to obey orders instantly, for their own safety.

"Excuse me, Your Excellency," Stefan said, "but a lot of orders are stupid. How, then, can that be for our own safety?"

"Well, Stefan, it's like your mother and father. They sometimes gave you orders that seemed to be stupid, didn't they?"

"I hear you, Bartalamyeh Fyodorevitch."

"But," I said, "they obviously knew what they were doing, for look at the fine fellow you've become, eh?"

Actually Stefan was a pretty hideous sort of person, an unpleasant peasant with sly, slitted eyes, a thief and troublemaker; which I guess is why the others laughed so heartily at my description of him as a fine fellow.

(Later I heard he was one of the ringleaders in a mutiny in which eleven officers were murdered and an entire White Russian unit deserted to the Reds; but, then, that kind of thing was quite commonplace in the civil war.)

That was the day we received orders to proceed seventy miles upriver to Seletskoy. As this was the supply base for the offensive, it was a confirmation that in spite of our total unpreparedness, we were still to take part in the attack. General Brzhtvh was already at Seletskoy with the other battalion.

Seletskoy was on the Emtsa River, which was a tributary of the Dvina. We found the wooden town packed with American soldiers, and I was pleased to run into an engineer I'd met in France, a boyish lieutenant by the name of Lin Halver.

However, things were moving so fast I didn't have a chance to chat with him for more than a few minutes. I had to rush off to Brzhtvh's H.Q. There were only three days to go before the attack.

His H.Q. was in a peasant log cabin. Even though he was sitting on the hot, tiled stove, the general was in a chilly mood that day.

"Your battalion is ready, Bandyeh."

"No, sir. The men haven't even learned to aim their rifles properly."

"Is all right. The Bolsheviks haven't either."

"We're hopelessly unprepared, General."

"So is everybody."

"It would be crazy to expect the men to—"

"I was not asking if your battalion was ready, Bandyeh. I was telling you."

"Oh."

"Is essential the Russians take part in this attack with the British, French, and Americans."

"I see. All right."

Brzhtvh nodded curtly, looking at me with his blazing eyes as if daring me to assume that our shipboard camaraderie entitled me to rely on his indulgence.

"Then let us get down to business." He spread out his map on the stove. The main thrust, he said, was to be along the wide road from Seletskoy through Kodish, toward Plesetskaya. It was to be made mainly by units of the American 339th Infantry Regiment, with Brzhtvh's other battalion in support, Brzhtvh commanding. My battalion, however, was to move not south but west, against the town of Emtsa, which was above Plesetskaya, on the railway to Vologda. Simultaneously, the Americans and the French would be fighting down the railway toward Emtsa from the north.

Our battalion's part in the affair was to be principally diversionary, to unsettle the Reds in Emtsa while the Americans and the French were driving southward into the town. The enemy strength in Emtsa was estimated at three thousand. Units of the Kazan Regiment had been identified there.

I indicated the road we would have to take, from Seletskoy to Emtsa. "What kind of opposition will there be along here, sir?"

"There are no reports of Bolshevik troops. Obviously, though, the road will be guarded. You will just have to probe ahead of your main force."

"What condition is the road in?"

The inevitable samovar was hissing softly in the corner of the cabin. Brzhtvh shoved himself off the stove and went over and drew off a cup of dreaded Russian tea. "Is passable," he grunted.

"It must be the only road in this area that is, then, after all this rain. Can I see the reconnaissance reports?"

"We don't have reconnaissance reports here, Bandyeh. We ask peasants. They said the road is good all the way to Emtsa."

"H'm."

His shoulders bunched up. "Please do not hum to me, Colonel Bandyeh!" he shouted. "Is best I can do!" He drove his badly bent beard at me. "This attack has been ordered in too much of a hurry! Attack, they say! But they cannot even bring up supplies on time!" His eyes were puffy with fatigue and exasperation. I could see that quite clearly, as his eyes were only two inches from mine. "I have machine-gunners without machine guns, mortars without enough shells, runners without boots, ponies without fodder, and now, battalion commanders without brains, it seems! Perhaps you would like me to walk all the way to Emtsa, to make sure is safe enough for you! Ah, what nonsense it all is!"

"That won't be necessary, sir," I said huffily. "I'll take a look for myself."

He stared at me for a moment, then leaned wearily against the stove and rubbed his hairy face in a hopeless way. "Just be ready to move west toward Emtsa on time, Bandyeh," he said, as if addressing an adolescent whose recent behavior—drooling, lip-strumming, having fits, and exposing himself—hinted at the faint possibility that the lad might not be quite all there. "I don't expect you to get more than a few versts along the road, but perhaps that will be enough to upset the Bolsheviks." He started to get angry again. "But please do not also worry me! You have little enough time even to reach the river north of Kodish where you will start from, without all this strange talk that you will see for yourself."

"I can do it in a few hours, General. You see, I have one advantage."

"That you are deranged?"

"That I can fly."

Brzhtvh glanced around quickly for a defensive weapon. Yes, it was true: I was deranged.

"In an airplane, General."

"Ha?"

"There are suitable British aircraft at Obozerskaya. If one of them can land at Plesetskaya, I can arrange to fly along our route within the next few hours."

"A reconnaissance by air? But—that is wonderful idea, Bandyeh. Is brilliant!"

"We've been doing it on the Western Front for four years."

Brzhtvh's expression iced up again. He didn't like being reminded that their Russian methods weren't quite as up to date as ours.

"Do you want me to reconnoitre your line of advance through Kodish while I'm at it?"

"That will not be necessary," he said curtly, burying his beard in a map. "I have all the information I need here. It was drawn by Peter the Great, so it is accurate." He glared up at me, daring me to deny that a map drawn by Peter the Great could be anything but accurate.

As we clumped unceremoniously into the Y.M.C.A. hut at Selet-skoy next morning, an unsettling hush descended. About a couple of dozen doughboys were scattered around at crude tables. They had been chawing, smoking, and sipping soft drinks when we came in. At the moment, their mouths were open and stationary. I couldn't tell whether they were staring in resentment at this sudden irruption of officers into their refuge from army madness, or whether they were just looking mightily impressed at the sight of the fat, morose major, the blank-faced colonel, and the tiny, handsome captain, all in their plutocratic coats—the two Russians in scarlet and grey, and the other foreigner in a giant, moth-eaten fur coat purchased in Archangel from an Armenian banker who had lost all his money in a card game.

Gradually the conversation swelled back to its former boisterous level, mixed with politely suppressed laughter. I peered through the fug with watering eyes. The air was so layered with smoke it was several seconds before I located Lieutenant Halver. He was four feet away, democratically sharing a bench with several of his men.

After weeks of spine-cracking labor, flinging up blockhouses all over the landscape, Halver's particular engineering company had been inactive for several days.

When he saw the three of us lurching through the maze of benches and bodies, his pleasant, alert features brightened welcomingly.

"Well, hello there," he cried, standing unsteadily. He looked flushed, and the top of his tunic was unbuttoned. As he and his men appeared to be drinking only ginger ale, I assumed it was the heat that was mottling his face. It was stiflingly hot in the canteen, and hazy with cigarette smoke and wood smoke from the stove.

"Hey, come on over and join us, Colonel."

"Just what we were hoping to do, Lin."

"That's great. Hell, I thought you'd be miles away by now. Move over, fellers. It's that guy I was telling you about."

His men looked me over cautiously.

"Lieutenant, I'd like you to meet Major Poupychev. Major Poupychev, Lieutenant Halver."

"Hello, there."

"And Captain Kisselev."

"Howdy," Lin cried, his face flushed with ginger ale. "Gentlemen, let me introduce you to Dave Swadge, Gil Leng, Art Stendardo, and Sergeant Bill Fine. Hey, Dave, see if you can rustle up another three glasses, huh? Say, this is great."

As we crushed onto the bench, the canteen manager, a young civilian with a pale, unformed face, watched suspiciously as Private Swadge weaved back to the table with his fingers stuck in three empty glasses.

"These gentlemen are American engineers," I explained to Kisselev in English. Kisselev smiled, though he hardly understood a word of the language. "And it's a well-known fact that American engineers are the best in the world."

"Oh-oh," Lin said. "Better fill 'em to the top, Bill. He wants something."

Sergeant Fine was clutching a bottle under the table in his huge, chapped hands. With extremely unconvincing nonchalance he glanced across at the manager. The manager happened to be looking away. Sergeant Fine drew a handful of glasses out of sight. There was a clinking and gurgling noise.

"All we got is ginger ale," Lin said, and winked solemnly as he pushed the half-filled glasses toward us. "Rules of the house, right, Bill?"

Major Poupychev looked mystified and uncomfortable. He wasn't used to hobnobbing with private soldiers.

Also, he was still in something of a tizzy, a pother and a stew over the new orders I'd been forced to issue immediately after returning from the aerial reconnaissance.

I'd made the trip early that morning in a Sopwith 1½-Strutter, a fine reliable 1916 aircraft flown by an equally fine pilot, an ex-Royal Naval Air Service toff in a white silk scarf.

It had been a triumph of airmanship, plucking the Strutter out of the mud at Seletskoy. He had flown there from Obozerskaya to pick me up, and had to make four attempts before he finally staggered into the air with about thirty pounds of Slavonic gumbo plastered to the undersurfaces of the wings and fuselage.

Thus encrusted, we had flown along the route that our battalion was supposed to take. But it had hardly needed more than a glance to determine that we sure as hell weren't going to get anywhere near Emtsa along *that* road.

Even under a badly-lit sky, you could see the light reflected in the troughs and potholes. The waterlogging was confirmed when we dipped down to 100 feet. The road looked, as the pilot expressed it, about as firm as a whore's mattress.

In places the outline of the road had disappeared completely in wild scribbles of mud where carts had got stuck and had had to be hauled out by brute force. A few miles past the theoretical front line, just west of Kodish, the water from a marsh had made things even worse by seeping onto the road, creating a sausage-shaped lake.

That was where the Reds had established themselves, and there was no way around them. There were about 200 of the enemy. They could have held the road with five cooks and a veterinary officer.

There was no way to get at them without wading straight into their guns. And I certainly wasn't going to do that.

However, while I was up I thought I might as well take a look at Emtsa. I bawled at the pilot and he banked the aircraft over the Red positions and continued along the road.

Emtsa was about twenty miles further on. It was easily identified as it was near the intersection of the Emtsa River and the Archangel-Vologda railway.

We circled the town at 1,200 feet, just under the clouds. From the back seat I hung over the side in the chill slipstream, studying the town and then the bridge a mile south, which was being held by a unit of Red Guards; then back along the forty-mile stretch of river to Seletskoy.

After three trips up and down that river, I decided that that was the way we were going.

"Is too shallow," Kisselev had protested.

"It's deep enough for the method I have in mind."

"The water flows the wrong way—we would have to travel upstream," Lieutenant Togonidze exclaimed.

"It's slow-moving even where the river narrows into channels."

"There are no boats available," Lieutenant Bodrov shouted. "Your Navy has withdrawn from the waterways, and the few barges and paddle steamers we have are needed to ferry the troops across the river at Kodish!"

"That's why we're going to see the Americans."

"You cannot countermand General Brzhtvh's orders!" Poupychev cried, in a panic.

"I haven't been able to get in touch with him. He's already left for the Kodish operation."

"It won't work!" Poupychev shrieked. "It is hopeless! We must do things the correct way!"

"This is the correct way. So cancel the move, please, and send the men back to their billets," I said, though I was well aware of the awful job I was giving him. It is extraordinarily difficult to get an Army machine to overcome its inertia.

The officers continued to remonstrate heatedly. Many of them already distrusted me because I was not only a mad foreigner but a pilot, i.e., somebody frivolous and irresponsible, fit only for bombing, machine-gunning, and drinking himself silly.

I finally had to stamp my foot at them and order them formally to undo all their good work.

I had acted like the very worst kind of despotic commanding officer, but it had worked. After three years in the Tsarist Army, they had grown used to autocratic nincompoops.

I became aware that Halver was nudging me.

"What's the matter with that gloomy major of yours?" he whispered loudly.

His men leaned over to listen, their faces looming sweatily out of the smoke and heat of the Y.M.C.A. canteen.

"He's in a huff," I whispered back, "because I've cancelled the general's orders for our attack."

"My guard."

"Just temporarily, mind you."

"Jesus."

"You see, we were supposed to be attacking along the road to Emtsa."

"Yeah, I know."

"But it's impassable."

"You're impassable too, Colonel. My guard, you can't just countermand a general's orders, just like that," Lin said excitedly. "Even if he is only a Russian." He looked around. "I told you he was crazy!"

"You didn't say he was crazy, Lieutenant. You just said he was kind of eccentric."

"That's right. Absolutely crazy."

97

"The thing is," I went on, sweating inside my tatty furs, "it would take a week to reach Emtsa by that road."

"Yeah?"

"Even if there wasn't a force of Reds half-way along it."

"Uhuh." Halver looked at me more calmly. "This leading up to something?"

"The point is that not only is the road impassable but so is the forest and marsh on either side."

"My, my," Dave Swadge said. He had a dark, cynical sort of face with a three-day growth of beard that made him look like a rather vicious gollywog. "You don't mean to tell me it's just like all the rest of this goddam countryside?"

"Yes."

"Gee, I'm really amazed."

There was a pause. Sergeant Fine, who had been studying Kisselev appreciatively for some time, suddenly put an arm round him and gave his shoulders a friendly squeeze. "Say, you're a neat little feller ain'tcha, Cap'n."

Kisselev looked at me enquiringly, but I didn't know how to translate this. Major Poupychev, who knew some English, stared bewilderedly at the big American.

"Ain't he the cutest, handsomest little doll you ever seen, though? Jeez, would my kid sister love him for Christmas."

"Put him down, Sarge," Halver said. "The manager's watching."

Captain Kisselev raised his eyelashes and his glass.

"Is visky?" he asked.

"That's right, little feller. Scotch."

"Scotch," Kisselev said. He gestured politely at the sergeant with his glass, breathed out noisily, brought the glass to his lips and drank the contents in one open-mouthed gulp.

"Ha!" he shouted, and raising himself to his full height of four feet eleven inches, flung the glass at the stove. It struck the pot belly with an alarming crash. Silver splinters flew through the air and pattered against the far wall.

"Uh . . . as I was saying," I said, after the manager, looking more suspicious than ever, had come and gone, "so—the road is out."

Wrenching his eyes off a now angelically smiling Kisselev, Lin said, "You're not thinking of moving your men upriver, are you?"

"Yes."

"Well, in that case you've substituted an impassable road for an impassable river. It's too shallow, even if there were any boats around, which there ain't."

"That's true."

"So?"

"It's a real pity, because it's flowing quite slowly. And it's almost unguarded, all the way to Emtsa."

"Sure. The Bolos know darn well they've nothing to worry about from that direction."

"Because it's too shallow for gunboats?"

"Yeah."

"Or steamers?"

"Sure."

"Or even barges?"

"Right."

"How about rafts?"

There was a silence. Kisselev looked around alertly at the staring faces.

"Rafts? Rafts? What is rafts?" he said.

"You told me most of your work is in building blockhouses and winter quarters for the 339th?"

Lin nodded, regarding me unblinkingly.

"Out of all the fine, straight pine trees around here. You said they were great for building blockhouses."

"Uhuh."

"I don't suppose you'd be equally adept at building rafts, I don't suppose?"

He stared up at the rafters with unfocused eyes.

After a moment, he said slowly, "You sure it's navigable enough?"

"Quite sure. It narrows to ten or twelve feet in places, but the water is continuous all the way."

After a moment, Halver said slowly to Bill Fine, "It would be a change after all those lousy blockhouses . . ." He looked back. "How many?"

"Enough for three hundred men."

"Jesus H. Christ."

"In the next twenty-four hours?"

There was an uproar from the engineers. Sergeant Fine got up, walked around the bench, then sat down again, expelling his breath. "You're right," he said. "He's crazy."

"Colonel Bartholomew W. Bandy . . ." Halver took another breath and leaned over. "Look," he said. "We'd have to fell about two hundred trees. We'd have to get them down to the river, size them, trim them, lash them together, caulk them—you'd need over twenty big rafts to move that many men and supplies. You expect us to do that in twenty-four hours?"

"I guess it is asking a lot."

Halver looked at his men. They looked back at him.

"Here we go again," Dave said hopelessly.

But there was a gleam in his eye.

Halver didn't manage it in twenty-four hours. He did it in sixteen, in one, sustained, backbreaking shift, working far into the night by the light of campfires. He decided that if the men didn't mind being a trifle cramped, we could manage with fifteen rafts, each approximately twenty feet long.

The last raft logrolled into the river above Seletskoy almost exactly sixteen hours after the first axe chunked into the first tall pine. And he threw in forty punting poles as well.

A Tinpot Generalissimo

By the middle of the night of October 14, we had reached the jumping-off point for the attack, just north of Kodish.

Though the main force, composed of units of the American 339th Infantry, of the Canadian 16th Field Artillery Brigade, of the Royal Scots, and of Brzhtvh's regiment, were not due to cross the river until dawn, we were supposed to have started westward from this point some hours earlier, as we had much farther to go, and theoretically were not supposed to be in touch with the enemy for the first ten or so hours.

So I instructed everybody not to stop but to keep going, giving as an excuse the fact that we were well behind the official schedule. My real reason, however, was to avoid a loud scene with General Brzhtvh. He would have read my message by then, and I feared that he might try to strangle me until my eyes fell out when he found I'd changed all his orders.

I realized later that he couldn't have cared less which route I took. He was just testing an amateur battalion commander to see how much of foozle, bungle, or boggle-de-botch he could make of things. I don't think he really expected us to accomplish anything, but it would be useful experience for us.

Safely past Brzhtvh at Kodish, I pulled to the side of the river and counted the moonlit rafts as they poled past, to see how many men had deserted. Fourteen of them gurgled past. I was very pleased.

"We've only lost one raft," I said, drawing my head down into my fur coat. The temperature had dipped below freezing. "Fourteen out of fifteen. Not bad, eh?"

"We are standing on the fifteenth, Colonel," little Kisselev said with an even littler smile.

I cleared my throat. "M'yes, of course," I said gruffly.

We pushed off again. Two hundred feet farther upriver we passed the empty barges on which the main force would be ferried across the river for the Kodish attack.

For the first few hours, we made quite good progress. By four A.M., I reckoned we had reached the bend of the river north-west of Avda.

From there on, though, the going was much slower, as it took time to maneuver the nine-foot-wide craft through the increasingly narrow channels. In places, the river was only a few inches deep. It needed only one raft to ground on the bed to hold up all the following rafts in a series of geometrically progressive delays. Between four and five in the morning we travelled less than half a mile.

It could have been worse, though. By seven A.M., we had reached the clear stretch of the river, where we were to assemble the platoon that was to deal with the Red outpost I'd seen from the air. The outpost, a simple log hut perched on a bank above the river, was occupied by only a handful of Red soldiers. It was one and a half miles ahead.

It was starting to get light as the last raft yo-heave-ho'd into a preselected clear stretch of water, and tied up along the densely wooded north bank.

It was quite a sight, as the sun rose somewhere behind the mist and cloud. The entire stretch of it seemed paved with wood, the rafts sparkling with frost. The air was sharp and still. Early birds darted silently in and out of the trees. A snowy owl on reconnaissance flapped across the river and was mobbed by a feathery dawn patrol.

The men seemed exhilarated by the adventure as they prepared a hot breakfast. (As it was misty, there seemed no reason why fires should not be lit.) As they waited for the hot tea, soup, and black bread, they cavorted about the rafts, talking softly but excitedly, and pretending to push each other overboard. They were obviously well rested, and in high spirits. Quite a contrast from the previous evening.

Part of the delay in reaching the jumping-off point had been caused by their unwillingness to venture aboard the necessarily crude craft. They hadn't liked the idea, at all, of teetering forty miles upriver on twenty-foot logs. They became even more reluctant when, at Seletskoy, they saw two of the rafts break away and start to drift downstream with about fifty of their comrades aboard, all of them lying flat on their faces and embracing the logs and wailing, too petrified even to stick in the poles and thrust themselves back to the river bank. The American engineers on the bank had laughed so much that one of them had choked on his chewing gum.

By the time we'd convinced the men that floating on a river was much more fun and much less arduous than floundering through mud and swamp, it was almost dark, and we were faced with the task of maneuvering fifteen rafts upriver with only the most rudimentary system of communication, i.e., by a system of hoarse whispers.

"Hello, raft just behind, this is number twelve, what number are you?"

"Twelve."

"How can you be twelve, we're number twelve."

"No, you're not, we're twelve. His Excellency said."

"His Excellency is *nyemsky*. He said *we* were twelve."

"Tell you what, comrade. You be twelve and we'll be twelve and a half."

We had hoped to creep up on the outpost by river, under cover of darkness, but it was almost full daylight before the platoon was ready to move.

As the outpost had a clear view down half a mile of river eastward, these tactics were no longer feasible, so we had to take to the north bank. It took over an hour to get through the last half mile of forest.

I'd put Captain Kisselev in charge of the assault platoon, emphasizing that I was just going along as an observer. So I brought up the rear, just in case some of the men decided to vanish into the arboreal gloom. They were showing marked signs of nervousness at the prospect of a fight.

As it turned out, only one shot was fired. When I went forward to join Kisselev I found that he had reached a shallow gully. It was all that separated us from the hut, which was barely a hundred feet away. The only enemy in sight was sitting on a rock at the edge of the river bank, shaving.

He was obviously supposed to be a look-out, but all the time we had him in sight he raised his napper only once from the piece of metal he was using as a mirror.

It was my first close look at a real live Bolshevik. He was wearing a greyish-green *rubashka*, something like a combination shirt, blouse, and tunic, and ragged grey breeches. There was a red star sewn on his sleeve. Apart from that last item, he was indistinguishable from most of the White Russians, including the ones in the Slavo-British Legion, who, though they had been outfitted in British khaki, had gone back to the usual cast-offs and rags. I think they were keeping the khaki as their Sunday best.

One of Kisselev's men excitedly aimed his rifle. Kisselev hissed and glared at him. The man lowered his weapon, grinning self-consciously.

As we watched from the blackness of the forest, another man came out of the hut, carrying a bucket. He went to the edge of the river and pitched the yellowish contents over the edge, yawned, stretched, called something to the sentry, then slouched back into the hut, scratching himself with the bucket.

Kisselev gathered his thirty men together, and whispered instructions. It was quite a touching sight, somehow, the tiny little captain surrounded by the hulking moujiks. Any one of them could have tucked Kisselev under his arm and still had plenty of strength left for his pack, rifle, and loaf of black bread.

As he finished whispering, Kisselev glanced across at me interrogatively, his long eyelashes spraying out from his alert, black eyes. I just gestured. It was his show.

We crept cautiously down into the gully, glancing repeatedly at the sentry until he dipped out of sight. His profile slowly appeared again as we rustled up the far side of the gully and crouched along the rim. The sentry was wiping his face with a rag, now, and humming to himself.

Kisselev looked along the line of men, took out his revolver, then stood up and swept his arm over as if slow-bowling at a rather boring cricket match. He climbed out of the gully, straightened, then strolled casually in the direction of the hut. As one of his men started to rush forward, Kisselev snatched at the man's sleeve, forcing him to a walking pace.

We were almost at the hut before the sentry turned and saw us. He gaped. Nobody moved for several seconds. As he snatched up his rifle, one of our men fired. The crack of the rifle echoed down the river.

As usual, the bullet went nowhere near the target, but it upset the sentry no end. He took a step backward and fell into the river.

Kisselev turned to face the hut, his revolver held out at arm's length. A few seconds later, six men ran out. When they saw thirty rifles pointed at them, they stopped dead and flung up their hands. They had all rushed out without their weapons.

A couple of minutes later, Kisselev, keeping the barrel of the Very pistol as low as possible so as not to attract attention upstream, fired a flare. The bright green light curved shallowly over the water and dropped into it with a puff of green smoke. It burned for a few seconds, then winked out.

It was the signal for the rest of the force to proceed. Five minutes later, the first raft cautiously peeked round the bend of the river, half a mile away. At the same moment, the faint thud of guns sounded from the east. The main attack through Kodish was under way.

Three hours later, we were in position for the attack on the railway bridge south of Emtsa.

Three of our companies, with Lieutenant Bodrov scouting ahead with a section, had taken to the north bank about a mile short of the bridge, made their way across a swamp, and occupied the wood just short of the field where the Red unit was still busily preparing its defences.

Simultaneously, Lieutenant Togonidze, who was in charge of the mortars, led a party along the south bank to a clearing about two hundred feet back from the river and more or less opposite the enemy camp. As soon as I fired the first Very light, they were to open fire, with all five mortars, for exactly one minute. The moment they stopped firing, the rest of us were supposed to come charging out of the wood on the north bank, with fixed bayonets.

As a plan of attack, it was simple to the point of idiocy, and the officers, knowing I'd been nowhere near a staff college and was totally ignorant of the finer points of tactics and strategy, were plainly uneasy, especially because I'd no alternative plans to meet unforeseen contingencies or setbacks.

It was true I knew nothing of staff-college stuff—military history and geography, economics, military law, and the like—but I had learned from a certain Captain Craig the value of speed and surprise in an operation of this sort. So I wasn't too worried about my dispositions. Provided the men, spread out in the wood on either side of me, clearly understood that they were not to move forward until the second Very light went up, the action, I felt, had a good chance of success.

The only thing that was worrying me was whether they would attack at all.

I wasn't at all confident about it. Even General Brzhtvh had admitted that there was little sign of dedication to the White Russian cause among the rank and file of the Slavo-British Legion. Moreover, there were not a few Bolshevik sympathizers among them, ready to exploit the situation at the first hint of hesitancy or failure.

Major Poupychev tried to reassure me. "The men would not dream of letting you make the charge all by yourself, Bartalamyeh Fyodorevitch," he said. "Already they would follow you anywhere.

"They like your jokes," he added gloomily.

But, then, adjutants were supposed to say encouraging things like that.

He was right, for once. It turned out quite well. A suspenseful half-minute after I'd fired the first red light high into the air, mortar bombs whistled over the river and started to explode all over the field in front of us.

The mortars did no damage whatsoever—I hadn't expected them to—but they had the Reds running around in panic within seconds. Their disorientation was complete when, as the mortar fire ended and the second flare went up, they saw nearly three hundred men charging out of the trees to their right, and slightly *behind* their trenches. For, of course, anticipating an attack from the north, their defence works were all pointing the wrong way.

They dropped everything and ran. As I scampered forward with automatic in one hand and Very pistol in the other, I was relieved to see that they were making instinctively for the protection of the town up ahead, instead of retreating toward the bridge and making a stand there.

So we secured the bridge without opposition.

The men were elated, and hugged and slapped each other on the back, bellowing like mad. One huge bearded fellow called Seriozhka rushed up and embraced me, and gave me two great smacking kisses, one per cheek.

"I say," I said.

More and more men crowded up to the bridge for their share in the celebrations. While waiting for the right moment to get them in order again, I fired the green flare to bring up the supply rafts, sent off a runner—Ufan—to tell the mortar party to get up to the bridge as fast as possible, and called a hurried conference of officers and NCOs. As they reported in, we were astonished to discover that we had suffered only two casualties, including one fatality, a man who had been hit in the head by a stray bullet, probably one of our own. The Reds had hardly fired a shot.

One hundred seventy-one of the Reds had surrendered. Like the White Russian soldiers, most of them were young peasants who had been more or less forcibly conscripted. They were obviously just as inadequately trained as our men. They talked quite readily when Poupychev questioned them.

Among the captured stores were two Maxim machine guns on wheeled mountings. Until then, we had had no machine guns at all. I had them placed at the far end of the bridge, in case enemy reinforcements appeared from the south.

Meanwhile, I thought, we might as well push on while the enemy was still in a state of shock and disarray, so as soon as the festivities had petered out and some sort of order had been restored, I set off along the railway track at the head of a patrol, cautiously, in case any of the fleeing troops had been rallied by their commissars and were lying in wait for us. There were no Reds visible, however, until we emerged from a shallow railway cutting and Emtsa came into view.

It was about a quarter mile farther on, just beyond a large, flat field of long, yellowish grass. The town looked even more drab and scattered than it had appeared from the air. A few stone buildings were visible, huddled around the railway station. The rest of the town consisted of churches, log houses laid out with no discernible plan, and a large cemetery.

Carefully folding and laying aside my fur coat, I climbed to the top of the railway cutting and crawled forward for a better view.

The Reds had obviously been warned. Gangs of them were hurriedly digging holes and trenches along the southern edge of the town. There appeared to be many hundred of them.

Through the glasses, I could also see additional hundreds of soldiers milling around the railway station in the centre of town. I wondered why. A Compagnie Internationale des Wagons-Lits express was hardly likely to come along.

Just how many men were there in Emtsa? One of the prisoners had said that fewer than a thousand of their comrades remained, the others having troop-trained northward the previous day to meet the attack of the Americans and French at around Verst 455. (Locations on the railway were marked in distances from Vologda, apparently; Verst 455 was therefore 455 versts from Vologda, or about three hundred miles.)

Even a thousand Reds, however, were several hundred too many for us. Also, there was some very ominous activity going on among those birch trees about two hundred yards to the left of where the narrow-gauge track drove into town.

The Reds had a battery of guns half-hidden among the trees.

By then, our main force were straggling up the line behind me. Kisselev and Lieutenant Bodrov came scrambling up the embankment, followed by a panting Poupychev. Bodrov was one of the more enthusiastic officers, a young, rosy-cheeked fellow with bright blue eyes above a little snub nose.

As they wriggled alongside and aimed their field glasses, I said to Kisselev in a low voice, "On the left—take a look will you, Alexander Nikolayevitch?"

His glasses jiggled about, then stilled.

"What kind are they?"

Kisselev looked again through his glasses, then: "They are fifteen-centimetre howitzers," he said calmly. "Very good guns when properly used."

"What did he say?" Poupychev said as he crawled up, breathing like an asthmatic buffalo. "They have field guns?"

"Howitzers. Five of them."

"Oh, shyit," Bodrov said. He had learned this word from one of the Americans—certainly not from me.

The Reds were busy hauling the guns around to face us. Until a few minutes before, the howitzers, narrow and thin-looking weapons with unusually long, slender barrels, had been pointing in the opposite direction.

We watched anxiously. The Reds were being pretty efficient about getting the guns turned around. I estimated that we had about fifteen minutes before they were ready to open fire.

I looked over the town again and tried to put myself in the enemy's shoes. They must still be in a state of considerable perturbation down there; otherwise they would have organized a patrol by now, to probe our position and estimate our strength. But they hadn't. Therefore they would have no idea what kind of threat they were facing.

All kinds of rumors would be circulating as well, and the rumors would be frightening, because inevitably the facts would be grossly exaggerated.

The Reds would also be feeling trapped. Psychologically adjusted to the idea of an attack by bands of aggressive foreigners from the north, they would be totally unprepared for a sudden onslaught from the opposite direction. They would be all the more alarmed because we had also cut off their line of retreat.

Yes, if I were the enemy, I'd be in a frightful froth.

I looked at my watch. There was still a couple of hours to go before dark.

"Well," I said, taking a deep breath, "if we're going to attack, now is the time to do it."

"Oh, shyit," Bodrov said.

Five minutes later, the men started trotting out of the railway cutting. They spread out left and right over the soggy field with a discipline and dispatch that I wouldn't have thought possible twelve hours before. As they passed, they shouted and waved, their soiled, whiskery faces alight with pride, and bifurcated with vodka.

They had no right to look up at me like that, with such affection and confidence. I was sending them in on a frontal attack.

I'd been in several frontal attacks myself since 1916, and every one of them had been cruel and disgraceful and useless, reflecting the utter paucity of imagination of the Western leadership. I had sworn long before that if, by some dreadful error or circumstance, I ever found myself in command of numbers of men, I would never, ever send them in on a frontal attack. Never.

But, gosh, it was amazing how one's perspective altered, once one became a brass hat oneself.

Of course I told myself that if there had been the slightest sign of organized opposition I wouldn't have sent them in so precipitately, with such shocking lack of preparation. Nevertheless, now that I was a great captain of men myself, suddenly frontal attacks seemed the perfectly normal and sensible thing to do.

I didn't even feel much humility or concern. All I felt was hypocrisy. For as I stood up there on top of the railway cutting, smiling and waving back in a sovereign fashion, I was simultaneously working out what action I would take if half of the men were cut down before they reached the town and the rest turned and bolted.

Now 4 Company was trotting up the track. This was the headquarters company, in action for the first time, under Captain Sysojev. They were to attack straight down the railway track. I halted them at the cutting and waited for Lieutenant Togonidze to finish setting up his mortars over to the right. He was doing so with a care and thoroughness that at any other time I'd have found most praiseworthy. But I was now in a great hurry to get the attack going before that battery of guns opened up. Howitzer shells were not particularly alarming if you were familiar with them. With their high, slow trajectory, they always shouted out plenty of warning. If the audience was experienced, that is. But many of the men had never heard any kind of shell rushing through the air, and I was apprehensive that it might unsettle them enough to make the attack falter. Any sign of hesitation would encourage the defenders to resist with greater determination.

At last, Togonidze was satisfied with the siting of his weapons. He then spent another two damn minutes adjusting the sights, to range on the howitzers.

I forced myself to stand calmly in the open on top of the railway cutting, expressionless and motionless, but jumping up and down inside. As the men spread out over the field, a few shots were fired from the town. One bullet buzzed quite closely overhead.

That, at least, was heartening. Not the stray bullet, but the fact that the enemy was jumpy, shooting off their rifles at long range.

One of the runners tugged at my sleeve, chattered, and pointed. The men on the right were starting to move forward without waiting for the signal. I could hear the thin voice of their officer, shouting and trying to wave them back.

Now the men on the left were starting to shuffle forward prematurely.

Well, I'd just have to make it official. I hurriedly pointed the Very pistol at the darkening clouds and pulled the trigger.

The red ball of fire left a curiously erratic white trail against the dark-grey clouds. The hundred or so men concealed in the railway cutting started to rush forward, their boots crunching on the loose gravel under the tracks. "Walk, walk, don't run!" I shouted. "Save your strength, lads!"

I wished I was going with them. But I had to see what was going on, and I certainly couldn't do that if I were down there in the long, yellow grass.

I wondered why the lenses of the field glasses were distorting the picture. Or, Good Lord, was my vision going, was I starting to faint from sheer nerves? Then I realized it was raining.

I wiped the lenses hurriedly and looked back at the howitzers. One of them seemed ready for action. Its long barrel was rising. Just as I was about to give Togonidze an imploring shout, one of his mortars fired with a sharp, hand-clapping sound.

One of the loaders, who hadn't covered his ears fast enough, stumbled about, holding his head and cursing.

The shell burst well short of the line of guns, sending up a billow of grey smoke. Togonidze ambled across and adjusted the next mortar, still taking his time about it. But his next burst was right in front of the guns.

Now Togonidze moved faster, and quickly adjusted the sights of the remaining three mortars. He stood back and shouted. The three mortars fired almost simultaneously. As Togonidze trotted back to the first mortar, smoke swirled among the trees a quarter-mile away.

By then the troops had covered over half the distance to the town. They were still tramping steadily forward over the wet, yellow grass and around the birch trees. The fire of the defenders didn't seem to be getting any fiercer. Through the glasses, I could see one party of Reds shooting from behind gravestones.

They hadn't had time to dig trenches. As they were in a cemetery, they were probably glad about that. As I watched, one or two of them jumped up and started to run off, deeper into town.

For a moment, a curtain of drizzle obscured the others. When I focussed on the cemetery again, it was deserted.

The mortar fire stopped. "Keep firing, keep firing," I shouted.

"We are now out of ammunition, Bartalamyeh Fyodorevitch," Togonidze called back, smiling and shrugging.

My heart bounced as machine-gun fire sounded from the town. A flat phutting sound, like damp firecrackers.

A few of our men were falling. But then the firing stopped, as suddenly as it had begun.

Twenty seconds later, the first platoons were level with the log houses on the southern outskirts of the town. On the left, Captain Kisselev's company was charging through the trees on both sides of the deserted howitzers. I could see him waving his men on, past the guns, deeper into town. He disappeared behind a house. We were in Emtsa.

Only one party of Bolos held out, and that for only half an hour. They had barricaded themselves into the grey stone administration building near the railway station, and as the first of the attackers appeared in the cobbled square, they fired through the windows with rifles and machine guns. Captain Sysojev was killed instantly.

Just as I got there, Kisselev, learning that one of the defenders was a commissar, stormed the building from the rear, using stick grenades. Like all the White Russian officers, he had a ferocious hatred of the hard-core Bolsheviks. His former colonel, a friend of the family, had been tied to a tree and disemboweled by several of them, while their commissar, a former ensign in the Imperial Army, had stood by, grinning.

Two minutes after Kisselev went in, half a dozen of the enemy ran out the front door with their hands up. Kisselev ran out after them and threw a stick bomb. As they lay screaming and writhing over the crimson cobbles, he went up to the one in the black uniform and systematically shot his face to shreds.

I don't know if it was because they were free of their hard-driving commissar—the Bolshevik commissars were a tough, ruthless, and dedicated lot—or because they thought Kisselev might start putting *them* out of their misery as well, but most of the thirteen hundred prisoners we took promptly offered to support the White Russian cause. I thought the howitzer battery commander went a bit far, though, when he not only volunteered to join us but to turn his guns around once more and bombard his former comrades farther up the line.

The Reds were no more constant than the Whites, it seemed.

On our side, we had thirty-one casualties, including eight dead. The booty was quite impressive. As well as the 15-centimetre guns, we captured thirty-eight machine guns, several mortars with ammunition, numerous Mosin-Nagent carbines, which were hotly competed for, a shedful of food, clothing, and vodka, a motor car, a large sum of Bolshevik currency discovered on the person of an absconding supply sergeant, and about one hundred thousand leaflets signed by somebody called Trotsky, apparently one of the more energetic leaders of the Red Army.

The Train

The following morning. Six forty-one A.M. in the Emtsa Municipal Building. A cluster of candles on an iron stand burning a yellow hole in the morning darkness.

So far, about half the officers had gathered in the entrance hall, murmuring hollowly and drifting about aimlessly like hung-over ghosts. Major Poupychev seemed the only substantial person present, his bulk further inflated with pride in the White Russian achievement in capturing Emtsa before the Americans and French were even half-way there. He kept thumping and clinking back and forth across the tiles, splashing merrily every time he crossed the wet spot where the freezing rain had blustered in through a broken window.

"But of course," he was saying, "our success was only to be expected. These Bolsheviks are obviously much inferior to our own troops. This Lenin of theirs will end up back in Switzerland, I assure you, if we do not hang him first. As we say in Russia, *The shoemaker should not make boots for his ox.*"

I was getting a bit fed up with these damned Russian proverbs. "Don't you also say," I riposted, "*Where is the hunter when the reindeer has its hoof in a pool of lava?*"

Poupychev stopped pacing and looked at me. "What's that got to do with it?" he asked.

I peered around, trying to count the uniformed wraiths around us. "Where are the rest of the officers?" I snapped. "I thought you called this meeting for six."

Poupychev, still looking at me a shade suspiciously, waved. "Oh, I'm sure they'll turn up sooner or later," he muttered. "They have a good excuse, Colonel. They were up all night, you see, drinking and playing cards.

"Yes," he went on, stroking the hilt of his sword, "there is not the slightest doubt that we shall be in Moscow by January, just in time for Christmas."

His eyes double glazed to keep out the chill of reality, he immediately transported himself to some Moscow mansion to gorge on imaginary caviar, strawberries, and kirsch, or swirl to the music of galleried minstrels, with ladies with bosoms indented with diamonds.

I looked at him in resigned curiosity, as he dreamed back and forth, back and forth across the tiled floor, his lips gleaming like two slices of calves' liver. Poupychev was wearing his best Imperial Russian Artillery uniform that morning, complete with spurs, sword, and gleaming steel scabbard, and three and a half rows of medal ribbons, including the Russian Orthodox Church Good Conduct Medal (very rarely awarded). He might just as well have been wearing a loin cloth and spats. He had no useful knowledge of artillery whatsoever.

I'd discovered this the previous evening when I asked him to take charge of the battery of 15-centimetre guns. He had smiled forbearingly and explained that as a staff officer he had been concerned only with grand strategy. "The picayune details," he said, "I left to others."

"But all I want you to do, Major," I'd said, stupid with fatigue, "is to lay the guns and see they are fired roughly in the right direction. You don't have to actually *hit* anything, you know."

"Lay them?" he asked suspiciously.

It finally got through to me: he hadn't even *seen* a gun fired from close quarters since sometime last century.

What with him and people like Count Snetkov, it was no wonder the revolution had come as a bit of a surprise.

It was after seven before the rest of the officers assembled, yawning and bleary-eyed. Whereupon Poupychev, believing he knew what the situation was, proceeded to summarize it.

Skipping such sordid details as supply, transport, communications, and reserves, he talked at great length about our strategic intentions. I listened quite interestedly. I hadn't realized we had any, until then.

Poupychev droned on and on. He was enjoying himself so much I was reluctant to interfere . . . No . . . to be truthful, I was beginning to feel the dreaded Russian inertia enveloping me . . . as if I'd been given lumbar anaesthesia . . . A few more weeks in this brooding land, with its fearful forests and fatalistic humidity and I'd be lying on a stove like a skillet, rusting away in melancholy, saying, "What's the use . . . If *Gospod* had meant me to survive, He would never have set my mattress on fire . . ."

With his inspiring words about a consummated counter-revolution, Poupy would have made a fine hypnotist . . .

It was a relief when one of the officers interrupted him. He did this by falling off his English shooting stick.

He sprawled in an icy puddle of water, which made him very annoyed.

"Yes, my dear Major," he snapped, plucking fastidiously at his wet breeches, "but I believe you have some orders for us. Well, let's have them and get it over with, my dear Vladimir Petrovitch."

Thank goodness, I thought, for at least one realist.

"So we can get back to our bridge game," the officer added. Then, indignantly: "I was having a run of luck, you know."

"I was coming to that," Poupychev said. "However, first: our immediate objective is to wipe out the Bolsheviks who are now trapped between us and the Allied forces to the north. Accordingly, as soon as all is ready, possibly even within the next two or three days, we shall move north to link up with the Westerners."

Next two or three days? Surely he meant hours?

"Thus, with our help, the Westerners will be able to continue their offensive southward. We shall, of course, greet them in Emtsa with a parade, and with our glorious Russian tricolor flying triumphantly above this very building."

There was an approving murmur. Somebody started to clap, but desisted when the others winced and held their heads.

"What is the situation to the south?" Kisselev asked.

"The local bureaucrats have informed me that there are no Bolsheviks to the south of us within thirty versts," Poupychev said, a shadow of impatience flitting across his moonscape. He didn't much approve of little Kisselev. Kisselev could be so un-Russian at times, so darned practical. "However, as soon as I get round to it, I shall send out a patrol to make quite sure that there is no danger from that direction."

"It is true, my dear Major," one of the platoon officers said, biting a yawn in two, "that we should have no difficulty in linking up with these Westerners. But surely that won't be necessary? One of the local girls, I forget her name, the daughter of some paltry official, tells us that the Americans have already reached Verst 445."

"That's a good idea," said another. "Why don't we just wait for them to arrive? No need for *us* to stir, is there?"

There were sounds of approval. The ones without hang-overs nodded emphatically.

"That is a good point," Poupychev said. "We shall certainly take that viewpoint into consideration."

"Well, if there's nothing else, I think I shall turn in, now," another said, yawning so exorbitantly that his jawbone crunched.

"Good idea, Mishka. Me too," said a friend.

"Er," I said.

They all turned and smiled with polite condescension, obviously bracing themselves for another of my encouraging pep talks.

Before I could ruin the general mood of euphoria, somebody else beat me to it. Ufan, his ragged greatcoat sparkling with ice, came stumbling into the hall, panting urgently.

He stopped, momentarily abashed by the stares from twenty pairs of bloodshot eyes; then thrashed his way up to me and wrenched at my furs, and started to stutter incoherently.

He was so agitated I couldn't understand what he was saying. Major Poupychev was kind enough to repeat it for me slowly.

Ufan's message was simple enough, heaven knows: an armored train was approaching from the south.

After a moment, somebody said uneasily, "Nonsense. There are no Bolsheviks within thirty versts. I have it on the highest authority."

"But I saw it," Ufan shouted, scratching himself frenziedly. "A big long train, with great big huge guns!"

"It's just as I thought," Poupychev said. "It's hopeless. We are doomed."

Because of the outrageous condition of the late commissar's almost new Renault, I had no compunction about driving it at top speed over the fields and crashing it ruthlessly over hillock and ditch. I found Lieutenant Bodrov and his sergeant at the south end of the bridge, near the Maxim machine guns. Bodrov was looking anxiously through his field glasses. The sergeant was looking for the nearest exit.

Ignoring a hubbub of frightened queries from the machine gunners and the pleading looks of the sergeant, I trained my glasses down the track. The locomotive was still about five miles away. It was headed straight toward us, so all I could see, fuzzily, through the draperies of rain, was its smokestack and the red flags crossed over its round boiler.

"There are twelve cars, Bartalamyeh Fyodorevitch," young Bodrov said, trying to sound nonchalant. "All of them are heavily armored. There are two big guns."

"Thank you."

"Shall I blow up the bridge, Excellency?" the sergeant asked.

"Just a moment."

"But we must do something quick, Your Excellency! It is coming very fast! There is no time!"

I looked back at the train, chewing my lip. I turned to Bodrov. "Is that true, Petya?"

"I agree. We have only a few minutes. The charges are laid."

"I mean, do you agree that the train is travelling fast?"

"The fuses are ready to light," the sergeant said helpfully.

"Yes," Bodrov said. He sounded short of breath. "I saw it clearly when it came round the bend. It is coming up at full speed. It will be here in perhaps twelve minutes."

"Listen, Petya," I said. "Are you listening?"

Bodrov took a deep breath, came to attention and thumped the heels of his boots together. "At your orders, Colonel," he said, his eyes wide-open and brilliant.

"Petya, if the train was expecting trouble, do you think it would go fast or slow?"

Bodrov stared as if I were trying to start a discussion on the merits of the Maryinsky Ballet. "If it were expecting trouble?" he said. "But of course it is."

"Then would it go fast or slow?"

Bodrov started to reply, stopped, then said, "It is true . . . They would not take risks with a valuable train."

"Does that not suggest that they are not expecting immediate trouble, if they are travelling fast? That they may not know we have captured the bridge—or that we are in Emtsa?"

"But they must," he replied bewilderedly. "Or why else are they here?"

"We must blow the bridge," the sergeant said angrily. "I ask permission to blow up the bridge immediately."

"Shut up." I turned back to Bodrov. "They may just have been sent up to reinforce their comrades north of Emtsa."

A soldier manning one of the machine guns nearby, started to run back along the bridge. I stepped in his way. "Get back to your post, you great, lousy bundle of rotting, evil-smelling rags," I said in English, but smiling and nodding at him encouragingly at the same time. The soldier hesitated, shuffled, then went back, trying to look as if he had merely been stretching his legs.

"You are going to assume they do not know we have captured Emtsa?"

"Sergeant Pazelsky was smart enough to cut the telegraph wires as soon as we took the bridge, Petya."

"It . . . it is a great risk," Bodrov said shakily, his fresh cheeks pink and hot enough to melt the ice that had formed on his fur hat.

"The other way is worse, isn't it?" I pointed down the track. "If we blow up the bridge, they will still be there. The train will dominate the town and the railway as far north as its guns can range. Also, blowing the bridge would be to their advantage. We wouldn't be able to get at them. What do you say, Petya?"

"It is a great risk, Colonel."

"I'm going to try it, Petya. Especially as *you're* the one who's going to take the risk."

Ten minutes later, from the safety of the railway cutting three quarters of a mile back, I watched through field glasses as the train reached the bridge, or, to be exact, a point about a hundred yards short of it. By dipping the glasses slightly, I could see our machine guns in place. But now they were both under the bridge. They were covering the hundred or so ex-Bolsheviks who were pretending to dig trenches in the field below the bridge.

I was having them covered just in case any of them got the idea of running for it and giving the game away, or warning the train that they were no longer loyal little Red soldiers.

The moment the train stopped, a dozen soldiers jumped off,

holding their rifles clumsily at the port-arms position. They were surrounding an officer in a grey greatcoat.

At least I assumed he was an officer, though his only insigne was his red star. From this distance, he looked about sixteen years old.

Bodrov, also wearing a red star on the sleeve of a *kittel* that he had hastily borrowed from one of the former Bolos, walked forward to meet the newcomers.

The view jiggled as Ufan clutched at my arm and whispered excitedly. I turned on him, hissing fiercely, then turned back to the train, agitatedly refocussing.

I couldn't locate Bodrov. For an awful moment I thought they had already seen through his bluff and promptly liquidated him. But then one of the Reds shifted aside and I saw Bodrov talking to the officer.

Everything now depended on Bodrov's not losing his nerve. I watched tensely, holding my breath.

Bodrov admitted later that he had been sweating and quaking so noticeably that he had to pretend he was suffering from some unspeakable disease. He said that luckily he hadn't needed to persuade the colonel in command of the train (after abolishing all commissioned ranks for several months, the Reds now appeared to have restored them) that Emtsa was still in Red hands. The colonel was so convinced that his enemies were still many miles away that he had asked only the most perfunctory questions about the local situation. His main concern was to get on up the line as fast as possible.

He had shown only a momentary suspicion. That was when he mentioned a name unfamiliar to Bodrov.

"Avilov, Comrade Colonel?" Bodrov faltered.

"Avilov. Surely you know the name of your own adviser?" the colonel asked with a frown.

Bodrov managed to conceal his momentary confusion. Avilov, apparently, was the name of the commissar Kisselev had killed.

In the meantime, I took the opportunity to study the train. From this angle I could see its entire length. The locomotive was apparently not Russian-made, for it lacked the usual tall smokestack. It was drawing a dozen cars, every one of them heavily armored with crude steel plates.

The second and third cars bore long-barreled guns. They looked like naval guns. In addition, there were several heavy machine guns on swivelling mounts on top of six of the remaining ten cars. The rear three cars seemed to be passenger coaches, the doors being almost undiscernible openings in the armor plating.

A formidable weapon, that train. With the doors secured it would be impossible to get at the occupants without a giant tin-opener.

Unless, of course, they were so obliging as to open them voluntarily . . . ?

We arrived back at the railway station only eight minutes ahead of the train. As the Renault squealed to a halt on the weedy ground alongside the track, a dozen officers ran up, shouting questions. Then swarms of NCOs and men surrounded the car. They were all looking at me as if I were Moses in a Red Sea that had failed to part.

On the far side of the cobbled square, Poupychev was also surrounded, in his case by equally disillusioned-looking civilians. The fattest and best-dressed of the civilians—he was wearing a sort of beaver hat, so coated with white ice from the freezing rain it looked like the first prize in a loony-bin baking contest—hurried over, waving his arms.

"Now see what you have done!" he shouted, stamping his foot and wringing his mitts. "We shall all be murdered by the Communists, or worse, robbed of all we have in this world!" He stamped his foot again. "What a calamity it is! What have we done to deserve it, that's what I want to know. It's disgraceful, that's what it is! Oh, what nonsense it all is!"

The rest was drowned in the panicky hubbub. I stood up on the front seat of the car, holding onto the windscreen. "Listen, lads," I bellowed. "Listen! The enemy doesn't know we have captured Emtsa! No, listen! Silence! Quiet! Shut up!"

"Listen to the comrade Colonel, boys," somebody called out—presumably a former Bolo. "Let's give him a chance, eh?"

"The Bolsheviks don't know we have taken Emtsa," I hollered, trying to sound calm as custard about it. "So listen to me, lads: we're going to make them think we are Bolsheviks! I want you all to line up along the track! You understand? Do just what you usually do when there is a train coming. Stand along the track and wait for the train to stop. Wait for them to open the doors."

The men fell silent, gaping. It took an effort not to jump up and down on the seat in exasperation at my own stumbling words. I'd had a thumping headache for days now, from concentrating so intensely on the language. Many times, I'd had to give up and let Poupychev translate.

But I had to get across to them now, and very quickly. I could hear the train. It was already chuffing into the southern part of the straggly town. Its smoke was visible, too, billowing up as if half the town were on fire.

Maybe it would be, in a few minutes.

"Isn't that right, Alexander Nikolayevitch," I bawled across to Kisselev. "It will seem more natural if the station is crowded? Is it not so that Russian *vauxhal* are always crowded with people, waiting for a train?"

It was elegant Lieutenant Togonidze who got it first. "That's right," he shouted, addressing the huge throng. "Our colonel is right, my dear fellows. He means that we must not hide and shoot at the train, but stand and wait for it, as if we are Bolsheviks ourselves. Then, when it stops and they open the doors, we will rush in, and kill them!"

The moujiks stared at him stupidly for a moment, then back at me, as if it were now my turn to talk incomprehensible gibberish.

Events were simply moving too fast for the poor old peasants. They were still looking apprehensive and uncomprehending as the quicker-witted among the NCOs started pushing and shoving and pummeling them into position on both sides of the narrow railway line—the only narrow-gauge track, I believe, in the whole of Russia.

The men were still thrashing around in hopeless confusion as the armored train appeared round the final bend, sending up clouds of dense, black smoke.

The train men, though, must have been reassured by the typical scene of Russian disorder. At least, there was no sign of hostile intent from them. Yet. And the train was perceptibly slowing.

As he leaned out of the cab, one hand on the controls and the other gripping the side, the engineer's face bore the usual expression of lofty contempt for the townspeople.

Meanwhile I was scuttling back and forth along the track, whispering, hauling, and shoving men into position, hoping nobody on the train would notice the few inches of khaki below my burly furs.

I found myself shoving the adjutant into position as well, and angrily asking him where the hell he'd left his rifle.

"Oh. it's you, Poupy. Where's your pistol?"

Poupychev waved it resignedly. "I shall give my life, of course," he muttered. "But it will never work."

"All the same, Poupy, *mon vieux*, you be ready to jump inside as soon as the doors are open— No, no, Doubevitch, no grenades! You'll just kill your own men. Damn it, you, don't point your gun! We must not look hostile! Oh, good Lord . . ."

I ran smack into Private Seriozhka and reeled back, cursing.

"But Your Excellency," he said bewilderedly, "if we just stand here they will kill us."

I explained again, hurriedly, between great shuddery gasps of apprehension and excitement. Seriozhka looked blankly at the train as it loomed out of the rain, spitting sparks. The great driving wheels grinded past, inches away. A gout of steam blew sideways, melting the ice on Seriozhka's *kittel*.

The train squealed onward through the jam of bodies, vast and ponderous, its brutal steel sides seeming to blot out the entire sky. I saw a set of grimy fingers wiggling through one of the slits in the side.

On top, the gunners were looking around, huddled over their machine guns. I couldn't tell whether they were on their guard or not. I glanced around quickly, to find out where Poupychev had sited our machine guns, but couldn't see them anywhere.

A few yards farther on, Lieutenant Doubevitch was talking quietly to an apprehensive platoon. At least *he* seemed to know what was expected of him. He was passing out bloodthirsty advice as he gripped an unsheathed sword. He looked quite pleased at the prospect of hacking off a limb or two.

A thought occurred to me. Seriozhka was still shifting about nearby. I grabbed his arm. "Kolya," I said. "Listen. Run to the steam —the—the engine! As soon as it stops, climb up and cover the two men there with your rifle. Do you understand?"

"I hear you, Your Excellency."

I could have kissed him with gratitude for this alert response. "Don't kill them, though. We need them."

"Yes, I understand, Excellency."

"Good. Go. Run."

Seriozhka lumbered up the track alongside the train, barging through the huge crowd. By now, the train had almost stopped. There was no sign of any of the iron hatches opening, though. God, it had to work now, or we'd be slaughtered. I looked around again for our machine guns. They might be desperately needed any second now, to deal with the gunners on the roof of the train.

I saw two of the machine guns. They were on the roof of the municipal building, two hundred feet away across the cobbled square.

I also saw something else. The tricolor was still floating above the roof.

The bloody idiots had failed to haul down the imperial flag.

"Oh, Jesus Christ."

Surely the enemy gunners had seen it. They were looking in that direction. It was too late to do anything about it now. The flag was plainly visible, flapping heavily in the freezing rain.

The train stopped with a prolonged nerve-twisting shriek of brakes. The soldiers on both sides of the track pressed back instinctively against the crush of bodies behind them, their faces tense as they fumbled with their weapons and stared wide-eyed up at the train, which seemed so utterly impregnable.

An agonizing pause. Nothing happened. Then, all at once, as if they'd rehearsed the action for a French bedroom farce, the kind where lots of doors open and shut simultaneously, the steel hatches all along the train started to gape. Faces and dim figures appeared in the openings.

The men around me remained frozen. I caught a glimpse of Doubevitch's sword, gleaming dully in the miserable light. Shouting, he ran up the steps opposite him, slashing away like a madman, and disappeared into the train.

Nobody was moving at the hatch nearest me. I forced my way through to it, through the men jammed against the steel sides. They were just standing there, as if waiting for an engraved invitation to board. I managed to get on the steps and forced my way into the interior, clutching an automatic. Then I was inside.

It was a converted cattle truck, packed with men. They retreated slowly to the far end, mouths agape, eyes stretched wide. Tired, bearded faces, little suggestion of a uniform, just an odd variety of torn, grimy blouses and filthy coats, dozens of different sorts of hat, boots, shoes, or just rags on their feet.

We looked at each other. The sound of firing farther along the train was muffled. Men shouting. A muffled bang from somewhere and a shocked silence, then cries of pain. Somebody using grenades.

"Out!" I said. "Out!" Nobody obeyed. I fired at the ceiling. The

Reds cowered, too frightened to move. For something to do, to impress them, I kicked at a teepee of rifles, scattering them into the straw.

Men crowded behind me. There was a deafening bang. One of the Reds shrieked and clutched at his chest. The rest flung up their hands and started babbling in terror.

It took minutes to fight my way off the train again. The machine guns on top of the municipal building were firing. One of them had tracer. As usual, they were aiming too high. I could see the wisps of smoke far overhead. The enemy machine-gunners were wrenching their guns around on the swivels.

Men were struggling along the entire length of the train, yelling. Guns banging, bayonets stabbing, grenades exploding among friend and foe. A stream of blood poured through one of the open hatches and splashed onto the icy gravel. Some idiot was firing his rifle at the inch-thick turret of one of the naval guns. The bullets howled off into the icy rain.

An iron ladder led to the roof of one of the cars. "Follow me, follow me!" I shinned up the ladder. The armor plating ended a foot from the roof. The wooden roof was more or less flat. There was a machine gun ten feet away. The gunners were trying to depress the muzzle to fire into the packed crowd on the far side of the train. I aimed. "Hands up!" The machine gun started to swing around. I pulled the trigger. The gun was empty. I couldn't understand that. I only remembered firing one shot. The machine gun was pointing at me. A soldier was wrenching at the loading handle. It had iced up in the freezing rain. It wouldn't fire. I threw my automatic. As it clanged against the gun shield I followed up, trying to get around the shield. I skidded on the icy roof. I cannoned into one of the Bolos. He rolled off the roof. Another Bolo picked up a belt of ammunition and flailed it. A couple of dozen 7.62-mm. cartridges clouted me across the head and I went sliding across the roof and over the edge, unable to hold on. Everything was coated in ice. I landed on Poupychev.

I was quite glad about that.

"Don't just lie there—get in there and shoot!"

"It's all over, Bartalamyeh Fyodorevitch."

"'tisn't! Don't be so bloody pessimistic!"

"I mean we have won," Poupychev said dazedly, and gestured —with some difficulty, as I was still sitting on him.

All along the train, in both directions, I saw arms held high in the air. Other Reds were still being hurled bodily out of the hatches.

The shooting had stopped. Men were shouting and cheering, waving. Whiskery moujiks were embracing each other, spitting joyfully.

It appeared that Poupychev was right. The fight was over.

Unfortunately, when I went forward to the locomotive, I learned that several of the men, maddened with excitement and blood lust, had stormed the locomotive, and despite the fact that Seriozhka was covering the crew with his rifle, had bayoneted the engineer and the fireman, killing the former and seriously wounding his mate.

So now we had a train, but among our fifteen hundred supporters, and this latest batch of about seven hundred volunteers, there was not one competent to drive the train onward.

Another View of the Train

"What happened then?" General Ironside asked.

"Yes, yes, tell him, Bandyeh, tell him!" Brzhtvh cried, shaking all over with excitement and bending his beard.

Ironside looked really interested, though he had already heard most of the details from the official reports, as well as personally (a talented linguist, he had picked up Russian in about three weeks) from several of the officers and men who had taken part.

I think he had insisted on first-hand reports of the action because of a perfectly understandable suspicion that most of the accounts he'd heard so far were products of the overheated Russian imagination. Brzhtvh's generous and enthusiastic version, for instance, had sounded pretty improbable, even to me.

"Well, there we were," I said, daintily heaping four teaspoons of sugar into my tea, "with a splendid armored train at our disposal and nobody to man it."

My lips pouted over the delicate rim of the Dresden chinaware. Forgetting I was back in civilization, or at least, Archangel, I sucked up a couple of mouthfuls. As the slurping sound splashed around Ironside's regal office with its curtains of purest silk brocade flouncing against fourteen-foot-high windows, I winced and tried to make up for the lower-class clamor by raising my pinkie; but had to fold it again when I noticed that there was dirt under the fingernail.

Ironside put a hand to his chin and turned to glance at Brzhtvh;

but the view in that direction was just as unrewarding. The great hairy Russian was trying vainly to insert the pipe-wrench of his forefinger through the handle of his tea-cup. Ironside swivelled away again, his handsome features twitching, and gazed out the window.

Outside, snowflakes were busy smothering the cupolas and onion domes of Archangel. It had been snowing heavily for two days, and though it was now midday, the sky was the colour of a gun barrel. Above the ermine roofs, the clouds wore a black lining, as if sending out invitations to mourn the passing of the sun. On the Troitsky Prospekt the trolley cars flashed startlingly in the deranged gloaming.

Even half an hour after arriving I was still looking in some awe at the Commander-in-Chief. Ironside was even larger than Brzhtvh, a magnificent giant of a man, at least six foot four, and weighing about 270 pounds, most of it brain and muscle. To make it all the worse, he was virilely handsome.

Nobody had the right to look like that, and be greatly admired by the rank and file into the bargain. I'd heard quite a bit about him in France. He was the only general, apart from Plumer, to have earned both the affection and respect of his troops, not least because he had frequently visited the front line, usually accompanied by his pet bulldog.

When he faced us again, he was still trying not to laugh at the two of us. "But you brought the train up to Verst 455, trapped another Bolshevik train, and linked up with the Americans," he said, looking at me as if in eager anticipation of a *risqué* story, familiarity with which would not diminish his continued enjoyment of it. "Then turned south again, to rout the enemy at Plesetskaya. So you must have found *someone* skilled enough to drive the train."

This time I managed to draw up a mouthful of tea with scarcely a sound.

There was a brief silence. General Brzhtvh suddenly sprang up, and with a laugh that Peter the Great might have uttered as he tortured his favorite son, smote me on the back.

"It was Bandyeh," he shouted. "Bandyeh himself drove the train!"

Time was still the crucial factor in this foray of ours, and that's what the others never seemed to grasp. When they learned that the enemy had thoughtlessly failed to provide a back-up crew for the train, the officers were immediately resigned to abandoning the whole idea of turning it against its former masters, and proposed instead a game of whist and a few parties before pressing on up the line on foot.

"Besides, we must reorganize, Bartalamyeh Fyodorevitch," Poupychev explained. "After all, we now have a considerable force to administer. With these latest volunteers from the train, we have nearly twenty-five hundred men. A real regiment!" And he went on to babble about logistics and a properly appointed regimental or even a brigade staff, a signal corps, a quartermaster's, an artillery staff—

"And perhaps a regimental band?"

"A band?" Poupychev pouted his bright red lips and thought about it—with growing enthusiasm.

"I used to play the drums, Bartalamyeh Fyodorevitch," Bodrov cried, his eyes lighting up. "I once had several tin drums, with which I used to accompany my collection of lead soldiers. I became so skilled that my grandfather, Prince Fomin, put an entire wing of the house at my disposal, so that I could practice undisturbed. Ah, what a good man he was. A real saint . . ."

"I myself play the balalaika quite passably," Togonidze drawled.

"Yes, well, perhaps we can talk about that later," I said hurriedly. I turned to Kisselev. "In the meantime, would you be good enough to select about eight hundred men you can rely on, Alexander Nikolayevitch, to man the train. And if Major Poupychev would divide the rest of the force between the town and the bridge?"

"But, my dear Colonel, you have just finished shouting that the train is now useless," Poupy said with a smile.

"I'll try and drive it myself," I said.

There was hearty laughter. Togonidze slapped me on the back and squeezed my shoulders affectionately. "You are a card [*dyestvyooshyeh*], Bartalamyeh Fyodorevitch," he said. "There is no doubt about it."

"Thank you. Please be ready to move in about an hour," I said, and lurched off up the track, my feet crunching loudly in the sudden silence.

A couple of minutes later, the officers appeared outside the cab and gaped up into it. I was already busy up there, looking knowledgeable.

I should like to have explained to them that when I was a boy I had often ridden the footplate of the CPR freight train that meandered daily from Ottawa to Mississippi Lake, and thence eastward to join the Grand Trunk Railway along the St. Lawrence near Brockville. The trainmen always stopped at the water tank outside my home town, Beamington, to swing their great fat hose over the tender. Sometimes they had allowed me to ride with them as far as Smith's Falls—where I sometimes had an awful job getting a lift back to Beamington. (For some reason, the engineer of the eastbound freight was rarely as accommodating as his westbound colleague.)

As I say, I should like to have explained this, but communication still took an inordinate amount of mental energy and I needed what little I had left to try to make sense of the controls that I was now gazing at so intently.

"It is impossible," one of the officers called up, looking irritated at this latest sample of occidental presumption. "It is quite plain from the superior way they behave that even real engine drivers do not understand the workings of a locomotive. Come down and have a drink with us, my dear Colonel, and stop all this nonsense," he said, gesturing around at the war.

"Besides, one should not tamper with fate," another said. "Look what happened to that fellow in Pushkin's *The Queen of Spades.* The officer in that story tampered with the unknown, and look where he ended up."

"Where?" somebody asked.

"I'm not quite sure, my dear fellow. My English nanny read it to me, but her accent was nearly as bad as Bartalamyeh Fyodorevitch's."

"I know that story," another put in and started to describe the plot. The officers all gathered round to listen with childlike interest.

"Seriozhka," I said.

Thirty minutes after that unfortunate bit of bayonet practice, the huge, lumbering peasant was still standing forlornly on top of the piles of wood in the tender, gripping his rifle helplessly. He looked miserable, as if he had been banished to Siberia . . . Except that, actually, he came from Siberia.

"You will be . . ." I didn't know the word for *fireman.* I picked up the stoking shovel and used it to swing the fire doors open. "Wood. Put wood on the fire."

"Then you are not angry with me, Bartalamyeh Fyodorevitch?" he faltered.

"I will be if you don't get a move on. The fire is nearly out."

His eyes shone. He scrambled joyfully from the tender. For a dreadful moment, I thought he was going to start smooching again. I hurriedly passed him the shovel and turned back to the controls, trying to ignore the growing audience of officers and men who were crowding the track on both sides of the cab, all making loud and unhelpful comments, except the one who was giving away Pushkin's plot.

The locomotive was obviously one of the few pieces of foreign aid that the former government had bothered to unpack. It was an old narrow-gauge engine, made, I think, by Baldwin, a U.S. firm, with six huge driving wheels and several smaller ones acting as hangers-on. Though it was old, it still had a great many levers, valves, wheels, and gauges, most of them scarred and bent as a result of repeated blows and knoutings. In fact, it looked not unlike the cockpit of a Dolphin, on a vast scale—and I couldn't immediately identify any of the controls, except the regulator handle.

Trouble was, though the Ottawa engineers had sometimes let me work the controls, I'd never really understood what they actually controlled. The regulator, for instance, that long bar sticking out sideways in the midst of the clutter: I knew it was the principal driving control, but what did it actually regulate?

Presumably, the steam entering the cylinders at the front of the loco. Let me see. The fuel, in this case large hunks of hardwood piled six feet high behind us in the tender, went into the sloping fire-box. The hot gases travelled around several miles of boiler tubing, and superheated the surrounding water to steam. This, under tremendous pressure, was allowed to enter the two driving cylinders. The steam exerted force on the pistons and piston rods. The rods were attached to the massive crossheads, which in turn were connected to the centre driving wheels by the main rods.

The power was thus transmitted to the wheels in a bicycle-peddling kind of operation, that is, by eccentric cranks. (And, having served in the 13th Bicycle Battalion, I was thoroughly familiar with eccentric cranks.)

So that was how a loco moved forward. To reverse it, the steam would obviously have to be admitted by the valve to the other side of the piston, pushing it forward rather than urging it back.

Right. Now. What was the right pressure for the steam?

Seriozhka was already stoking with vast enthusiasm, grinning all over his stubbly face. So the pressure would be rising fast. But to what? Think. It would be rather humiliating if I blew up the boiler before we even got under way.

Look, there was the pressure gauge, high up on the extreme right of the cab, above the car-heating steam-pressure gauge. Thank the Lord they hadn't changed the Western measurements. I'd have difficulty enough remembering the figures without having to transpose them from poods, or whatever system the Russians used.

Eighty, was it? Ninety pounds per square inch?

I put that problem aside for the moment, and turned to the cut-off indicator, marked in percentages. What percentages had the Ottawa engineers held it at? I couldn't remember that, either. Twenty-five per cent? Forty? And percentage of what? And what, in addition, did it cut off?

Then there was the reverser. There, the screw-reversing handle low down on the left. In spite of its name, though, it didn't necessarily do any reversing, did it? I seemed to remember that the Ottawa engineers had always set the lock in full gear before starting off forward. Yes! They'd told me once. It governed the timing and admission of the high-pressure steam in the cylinders. Subsequently, the engineer would turn the handle of the reversing gear to adjust the exhaust sound to his liking.

Perhaps that, then, was the cut-off, the percentages indicating the proportion of high-pressure steam being allowed to enter or exit the cylinders, to adjust for an economical pressure.

Then there was the water-level indicator. The water had to show in the glass but neither fill the gauge nor drop out of sight. There wasn't any water in it at the moment. What did that mean?

"Anyway, this chap Hermann—or was it Tomsky?—makes his way into the countess' boudoir," a voice was saying excitedly from the track alongside the cab, "and watches her from behind a screen as she undresses. The sight almost makes him sick—I remember that part—because the countess is over ninety years old. Anyway, as soon as she flings herself into bed . . ."

Seriozhka was still hurling tree trunks and things into the fire with joyous abandon, his ragged blouse already soaked with sweat, from exertion, and the increasing heat of the fire. But most of the wood was going into the nearer end of the fire-box.

"You have to throw the wood far inside," I explained hurriedly. "It has to cover the floor of the . . ." Fire-box. What was the Russian for that? "I'll show you," I said. And showed him by showering a shovelful of wood all over the floor, after completely missing the fire-door opening.

Red-faced—from the heat—I tried again, and wasted another two minutes straightening the edge of the shovel after it had clanged against the iron door.

"Yes, well . . . carry on," I said, and stared woodenly at the isolating cocks for the vacuum ejector, and wondered what the hell *they* were for, as well.

Several of the officers, who had presumably lost interest in Pushkin, were now crowding the steps of the locomotive, peering squeamishly into the sordid interior.

"Listen," I shouted exasperatedly. "You have fifty minutes left to get the men onto the train. Move! Quick-quick!" And to show them I meant business I yanked at what I thought was the whistle stop valve, to sort of underline the gravity of the situation with a dramatic ululation of steam. But all that happened was that a glass jar of scalding water emptied itself onto my foot.

I danced round a bit. However, they must have thought I was throwing a tantrum, for after a final, stupefied look into the proletarian interior, they started to retreat back along the track, whispering to each other in a mystified sort of way.

I stopped prancing as I suddenly remembered the water-supply valve in the tender. In a panic, I darted my eyes all over the place, looking for the valve. Maybe that was why the water wasn't showing in the glass. I was firing up a waterless boiler? No, there it was, on the tender. It was on. And the pressure was rising. Good God, it was already over 170 pounds!

I started to clutch at Seriozhka, then looked again. Of course! The pressure at which the Ottawa train men had maintained the boiler while it was drifting was 196 pounds. Higher only if they were approaching a gradient.

Good. That was one major problem out of the way.

Seriozhka was still stoking with undiminished enthusiasm, grinning hugely whenever he caught my eye. Steam was starting to wisp and snort from sundry valves, cracks, and crevices all over the locomotive. I leaned out of the cab, wishing I had an oily rag. Train engineers always had an oily rag to wipe their hands on. A couple of dozen tattered soldiers were still hanging around, though some of them were starting to retreat as the loco spat at them and dripped boiling water.

One of them was the sergeant who had had the presence of mind to cut the telegraph wires as soon as we'd taken the bridge. He was a former member of the crack Preobrazhensky Regiment and had still not got out of the habit of receiving orders without organizing a friendly debate on whether they should be obeyed or not.

"Sergeant Pazelsky!" I shouted. "Undo the engine! Unjoin the engine! I want to try it out, understand?"

He nodded, and instantly seized two of his men by the scruff of the neck. Bellowing orders and pointing at the coupling, he hurled them in between the tender and the first armored truck.

They immediately ran out the other side, and scuttled off in the general direction of Siberia. Cursing, Pazelsky had to unhitch the engine himself.

The pressure was now at 185 pounds, and the water was filling the glass gauge. I tried the reverser, but couldn't move it. For some reason, the designers of steam locomotives always made the controls stiff and heavy to operate, except for the regulator. The Ottawa engineers had spent half their time belaboring everything in sight with their picks. So who was I to go against tradition? I hit the reverser with an axe, and chipped away at it until it was at full lock.

Well, this was the great moment. I reached for the regulator, and taking a deep lungful of burning wood smoke—two lungfuls, in fact—pressed it down gently.

Seriozhka stepped back in alarm as the loco shuddered. There was a screeching sound. But nothing else seemed to be happening. I peered at the ground outside, to see if it was moving. It wasn't. I pushed the regulator down a little farther. The screeching got worse, and the loco vibrated alarmingly.

The engine started to move, grinding horribly, but at only one mile an hour, though the regulator was now nearly half-way down. There was something wrong somewhere. I felt sure that even a loco as old as this was bound to do more than just 1 m.p.h. at half speed.

Seriozhka had stopped feeding the fire. He was now looking decidedly apprehensive as the loco shuddered and squealed in agony. He had left the fire door open. The glare from the box showered him in brilliant yellow light. He had his hands over his ears and was looking ready to abandon ship.

I was ahead of him. I was already poised on the outside steps, with one leg in the air.

I couldn't understand what was wrong. The noise was terrible. It sounded and felt as if the loco had abandoned the rails and was trying to drive though a scrap metal yard on square wheels.

Down below, soldiers were gathering in multitudes, looking as if they felt they ought to be paying to watch.

The brakes, for gosh sakes!

Quick, where the hell were the brakes? One of the small wheels on the left of the cab had a steam valve above it. That might be it. I took the axe and hacked at it. The squealing started to die away. As the wheel jerked around under the hail of blows, the loco rumbled and picked up speed. In a few seconds, the driving wheels spinning and the exhaust beating like a thousand hang-overs, it was soon doing five miles an hour. Then seven. Then eight.

The axe fell from my shaking hands. But, by George, we were moving. I leaned exhaustedly out of the cab, face flushed, forehead beaded, eyes staring, to make sure there was nobody on the track.

There wasn't. But about a hundred yards ahead there were switches, where the siding joined the main line. My God, if they were open . . . I jumped back to the regulator and knocked it up, then grabbed the reverser. Having got the beast moving, I was now desperate to stop it.

The reverser was immovable. I wrenched at it until my veins stood out like blue snakes. It wouldn't budge. I looked around frantically for the axe. It had fallen off the footplate.

I leaned out of the cab and shouted down the line, "Axe! Axe! Get me axe!" Then staggered back to the brake, and, making perverted keening noises through clenched teeth, wrenched at it again. I could just see us hitting the switches, now only a few yards away, and continuing on over the track for a while, the loco bumping a bit as it left the rails and sliced a few ties in two, before finally keeling over in a dead faint, with me underneath.

Sergeant Pazelsky, meanwhile, was chasing after the loco, brandishing the axe in much the same manner as he'd chased his company cook after he caught the son of a yak spitting into the borsht for good luck. The loco was coasting quite slowly, but the momentum was still carrying it toward the switches.

Then we were over them. Apart from the usual rhythmic clatter, nothing happened.

So I continued to panic. It was like the first time I ever flew the Sopwith Camel. The moment the wheels left the ground, all I could think about was getting safely down again, so I could abandon aviation for something comparatively placid, such as submarine warfare. In much the same way, I just wanted to get that train stopped so I could lie down and tremble uncontrollably for a while.

Abruptly I was thrust aside. I almost followed the axe overboard. Then Seriozhka was grasping the brake wheel and twisting it in his huge hands.

There was a spiteful hiss, then a grinding, and the loco began to slow.

It stopped with a protesting yell about two hundred yards past the switches; which, of course, had been in the right position all along.

Getting back was much easier. I was very careful to operate the power reverse mechanism, take off power, loosen the reverse wheel, and apply the brakes in plenty of time. I certainly wasn't going to disgrace myself by driving too fast and damaging our precious train. So we crept back to the armored coaches at a ridiculous speed. It seemed like 1 in.p.h. The loco connected neatly with the bumpers.

There was an ear-splitting crash. The impact knocked over four hundred men, causing quite a few bloody noses, and sent me flying into the woodpile.

However, after removing the splinters and after some more practice along the rails, I was sure I was getting the hang of it. I ought to have known better. While it was not all that difficult to move a ten-wheeled monster by itself (once one had the brakes off), it was a totally different matter moving it with twelve enormously heavy cattle trucks, converted flat cars, and passenger coaches attached. With the pressure just right, at below 200, and with the brakes firmly off, and the water just so in the glass gauge, the train refused to budge an inch.

Even with the more delicate adjustment of regulator, reverser, and live-steam injector, the six huge driving wheels merely spun impotently on the rails.

I simply couldn't get the swine to move. To make it even more exasperating, the men, who had taken half an hour getting onto the train, kept climbing out again and walking forward to see what I was going to do next. Also, half the population of Emtsa turned out to watch as well.

They probably hadn't had so much fun since the 1905 executions.

To top it off, the freezing rain continued to fall, making it just that much harder for the wheels to grasp the icy rails.

I tried reversing. Naturally this worked spendidly. The whole train clanked backward quite effortlessly. But that wasn't the direction we were supposed to be going in. But when I braked, then tried to move forward again, the wheels did their spinning act once more.

Finally, by backing the train nearly half-way to the bridge, I found a slight gradient, just enough to get some kind of forward momentum. By teeny little movements on the regulator and with the reverser just off full lock, the speed gradually rose, and we were doing a good 4 m.p.h. by the time we reached the railway station again.

Twenty yards past, the wheels started spinning, the train stopped, and the passengers got off for lunch.

"Altogether," I told General Ironside, "it took three and a half hours to travel thirty feet. I thought I was doomed to remain in Emtsa for the rest of my life. I didn't particularly fancy that, as the local mayor, or whoever he was, was trying to present me with a bill for all the damage we'd done to his admin building."

"How did you finally manage it?"

"After the men had had a hot meal, I got some volunteers to collect everything they could find—ashes, gritty slush, cinders, stones, even pieces of cloth and fur and broken glass, and got them to lay the stuff on the rails in between the wheels, and ahead of them. And after some more jiggling, the locomotive finally got moving.

"Some of the men didn't get back on the train in time. I think we left about ninety of them behind. But I was darned if I was going to stop for them, or even slow up. I just kept on going, opening up an inch at a time. We got to Verst 445 in about an hour."

There we ran into the Red Guards, literally. Poupychev's information, of course, had been incorrect. The Allies were still at Verst 455. However, the appearance of the armored train in the wrong hands had its effect. My trainsmanship helped considerably. I collided with their troop train with such force that their forward cars were derailed. With their transport out of action, some of the Red Guards, following a brief skirmish, fled into the pine forests, and the remainder ran to surrender to the Americans, farther up the line. Apparently, after one look at the wild, blackened face staring at them from the cab, they thought they'd be safer in American hands.

"Unfortunately," I said, "hitting their train that way blocked the line to Archangel, so we couldn't go on. We had to go the other way."

"So you resumed the offensive southward, and continued on for about forty miles."

"Yes, sir."

"And took Plesetskaya the same day."

"Well, I thought we might as well. There was nothing in the way until we got there."

Ironside jumped up and strode up and down excitedly, smacking a fist into his palm. "Their main base—the only remaining strong point guarding the Trans-Siberian. You could have been astride the Trans-Siberian Railway in another day!"

"There wasn't enough follow-up support. We'd have been cut off."

"I know, I know. The usual story."

"I could not get past Kodish," Brzhtvh said, looking guilty. "The road was too bad."

"And all together," Ironside said, sitting down again, "counting the attack on the bridge, the capture of Emtsa, and the storming of Plesetskaya, you had, I believe 222 casualties?" He looked at Brzhtvh, shaking his head; "222 casualties. After a sixty-mile advance over the most difficult terrain I've ever come across. Four thousand prisoners, most of them now on our side. A huge amount of war supplies. A battery of howitzers. An armored train, a troop train—all in four days. With three hundred men."

"I told you he was not ordinary man," Brzhtvh shouted. "Ha?"

"No," Ironside said, looking at my horse face, as I snorted faintly and pawed the carpet with a Shackleton-booted hoof.

"Even though he disobeyed my orders, the devil!" Brzhtvh bristled, wrapping an arm round my shoulders and grinding my scapulas together. "Eh, you devil?"

"It was a superb achievement," Ironside said. "Tell me, Bandy, how do you account for it? Are you a student of military history and strategy, perhaps?"

"Heck no, sir, I don't know the first thing about all that stuff. I've just been around enough to notice that if there's one thing an army can't stand, it's somebody who moves at anything faster than a snail's pace. I don't think there's much of an achievement in realizing that. We just kept surprising them, that's all."

A couple of days later, I was back in Ironside's office at Army H.Q.

"Bandy?"

"Sir?"

"If you were in command in this peninsula, how would you conduct future operations against the Communists?"

"Eh?" I said. Then: "I don't want the job, sir, thank you very much," I said quickly. "But thank you very much for offering it, sir."

"I wasn't offering it. I was asking for your opinion."

"Oh," I said. "Well . . ."

"Bearing in mind," Ironside said, leaning forward and looking at me with hard eyes, "the supply difficulties, the obdurate attitude of the White administration, the approach of winter, political reservations at home, the fact that half the Americans are down with flu and three quarters of the White Russians are down with mutiny—I want your unbiased opinion about my decision to go on the defensive. What would you do in my place?"

I tried smiling at him obsequiously. When that didn't work, I said, "I'd attack."

"You'd continue the offensive deeper into Russia?"

"Yes."

"Like Napoleon?"

"These Bolshevik swine," I said, "may be good at slaughtering civilians—at Plesetskaya we found some people who'd had their hands plunged into boiling water, so the Reds could amuse themselves by stripping off the skin—"

"The Whites have committed atrocities as well."

"Not just because their victims were property owners."

"Go on," Ironside said grimly.

"The Reds obviously haven't the fervor to fight for their ideas," I said, with the first certainty I'd felt since arriving in Russia. "State ownership indeed. They'd make civilian life even worse than the army.

"Anyway, I'm sure the whole rotten Russian Revolution will collapse within the next few months. And we can help it along if we keep up the pressure. I'm quite sure of it."

Ironside glared for a moment, then suddenly smiled and came round the desk and drew up a chair. It groaned pitifully as he sat on it. "Well, I'm glad you see it that way," he said mildly, "though I don't necessarily agree with you." He studied his boots for a moment, then: "I've been in contact with the Air Ministry, by the way, about that appointment . . . They seem—well, pretty ambivalent about you, Bandy."

"Ah," I said, looking pleased about it—but not too pleased, just in case 'ambivalent' meant something uncomplimentary.

"On one hand they seem curiously disappointed over your success, and thoroughly annoyed to be hearing about you again. While on the other hand they seem to find it equally difficult to let you go."

"Like a piece of flypaper."

"Rather like a hunk of metal," Ironside said, "and they can't decide whether it's made of lead or gold." He regarded me unblinkingly. "Which is it, Bandy?"

"It just looks like gold. Actually it's brass."

"M'm. Yes, that's just the kind of answer I was expecting. Do you know, Bandy, I may be the first person ever to see through you."

"Oh, crumbs."

"I think you've spent your entire career trying to make people think the very worst of you. Presenting yourself in the worst possible light, out of a profound sense of the absurdity of human endeavor."

"Absurd? Me?"

"And naturally people have taken you at your own estimation, and believed most of the things you've said about yourself. But whatever its true—shall we say extrinsic?—value, your achievements in this war have obviously been considerable. In many ways, you're a great man, Bandy." He paused. "Do you believe that?"

"Indubitably, sir."

"I see you don't, but I've taken the trouble to look at what you've actually done, rather than listen to what you say you've done. You have many flaws, of course. But in the—"

"Flaws? What flaws? *I* haven't any flaws."

"Obsessiveness, arrogance, narrow-mindedness—"

"Oh, *those* flaws."

"Blind stubbornness, vindictiveness, deceit, disobedience, eccentricity—"

"Eccentricity? I think I resent that."

Ironside laughed. "Anyway, that's enough of Ironside's fireside homilies," he said. He got up, his smile fading. He glanced at his watch, his voice turning dismissive. "The appointment is confirmed, by the way. I'm giving you the so-called 2nd Slavo-British Division . . . though it's hardly more than a brigade at present . . . You'd better see Major Wedge about your orders and warrants . . ."

His voice trailed away as he busied himself shovelling papers off his desk and into his briefcase.

I stood to attention, then trudged toward the door.

"General?"

I looked over my shoulder before realizing he was talking to me. "Eh?"

"Are you still interested in the Guardian Angel?"

It took me a moment to adjust to this. "The parachute? Yes?"

"Just thought you might like to know about it. I gather you had some interest in the subject at one time. They're issuing to the squadrons on November fifth."

"Next year?"

"This year. November 1918."

"Ah," I said.

And, for the first time, it occurred to me that what Ironside had said was true: that human endeavor is pretty absurd, after all.

Home

As I stepped off the train at Ottawa, a brass band crashed into triumphant melody. As the introductory chords oompahed among the girders, a cloud of goitrous pigeons whirred through the steam and grit, defecating in panic.

An important-looking khaki-clad figure stepped forward. I put down my emaciated valise and drew on a world-weary and rather bored expression appropriate to my military eminence. Feeling very august, though it was only May, I straightened my shoulders and started to bring my hand to the salute, but faltered a bit when I noticed that the chap wasn't wearing any trousers.

Not only that, the fool was going in the wrong direction. He was headed toward some other passenger, at the far end of the railway car.

Then I saw he was, in fact, wearing pants—short pants. He was a boy scout—a fifty-year-old boy scout—with his whistle dangling—and the band was also in shorts and kneecaps.

It was the Manotick, Munroe and Hildasville Boy Scouts Band, and they were greeting the new Dominion Commissioner, Mr. J. W. Robertson, C.M.G., LL.D.

I cleverly converted my salute into an arthritic sort of wave, and sidled past through the mob, gazing far afield, feet and eyebrows raised and mouth slightly agape, to suggest that I'd just caught sight of my friend in the distance—obviously a rather shy and retiring

friend, as he had retired half a mile down the platform to skulk behind several crates of live chickens.

As soon as I was out of sight, I resumed my normal expression,
and, thus scattering farmers' wives in all directions, hurried for the
exit and Constitution Square.

For, of course, there was nobody there to greet me, behind the
poultry or anywhere else. This time there would be no newspaper
reporters, women's clubs, civic receptions, and small boys goggling.
Which was perfectly understandable, as it was 1920.

Everybody else in the Armed Forces had long since been demobilized, had settled down in civvy street, and had conceived
about a quarter of a million howling kids, if it is possible to conceive
of a quarter million howling kids.

Even the Militia and Defense representative on the new Air
Board didn't know who I was.

"You've just come from Russia? What on earth were you doing there?"

"Intervening."

"You don't seem to be on the strength of the Canadian Air
Force. In fact, we've no record of you whatsoever. Can you explain
that?"

"I don't know anything about a Canadian Air Force. I was in the
R.A.F. Then attached to the British Army. Though, before that, of
course, I was in the Canadian Corps. Before I was in the R.F.C.,
that is. Except for the time I was with the White Russians."

"Haven't you forgotten the Navy?"

"Funnily enough, an admiral did say once that he just wished
he could get me in the Navy. Matter of fact, he said it twice. That
was when I was at the Air Ministry."

"You were with the Ministry too, were you?"

"Just before I joined the 13th Bicycle Battalion."

"And just what was a pilot doing with a bicycle?"

"Peddling."

"I see. I see. Excuse me a moment . . .

"Just stand there, will you, Corporal. No, I don't think that will
be necessary, but keep it handy, just in case . . . The fact is, nobody's ever heard of you, Bandy—if that's your name. Can you
prove who you are?"

"I could ask my father, I suppose."

"I mean, who you are in the Services?"

"There's that letter from the High Commissioner in London. Everything else, my Identification Card, paybook and so on, was taken from me in Rush—"

"All that letter proves is that you told them in London the same story you're telling us. They're rather a gullible lot over there."

"Excuse me, sir."

"What is it, Mitchell?"

"Miss Arsenault has just found these newspaper clippings in the archives."

"In the what?"

"That tin box, sir."

"Oh, yes."

"There's quite a lot about a Colonel Bandy."

"H'm . . . You seem awfully young to be a general, Bandy. You only look about thirty-five."

"Actually I'm twenty-six."

"Are you sure this is you, in these clippings? You don't look like this now."

"Well, I . . . I was seasick."

"H'm. It's all very irregular, Bandy. Surely you must have *some* idea where your service records are?"

"Whatjamean? That's *your* responsibility, not mine. Look, all I'm interested in is getting demobbed, like everyone else."

"Demobilized? Why didn't you say so? That's an entirely different matter.

"Oh, good."

"That clears it up entirely, my dear fellow."

"Fine. So—demobilize me."

"Certainly not. You'll have to see the Soldiers Settlement Board, or somebody. That's not our department at all."

I'd gotten home so late that even the military were reluctant to get involved in the aftermath of the war—and I was an aftermath if ever there was one.

As for the civilians, judging by the looks I received from the bowler-hatted veterans, the impatient glances of the young women as they rasped past in their fascinating black and white silk stockings, and the annoyed hootings of the motorists on Wellington Street in their unfamiliar designs of motor cars, the country was determined to forget the European catastrophe utterly, and get on with the important things, such as mortgages and sex.

I was a nasty reminder of the conflict, for I was still wearing the all-too-familiar cloth the color of horse-dung; worse, it was the conspicuously ornamented uniform of the class that had made such a shambles of the war: bloody red tabs and overbearing braid, and the pip and crossed sword and baton of my rank rank.

No wonder the civvies glared. It must have looked as if I were flaunting my martial proclivity. They were not to know that, having returned from Russia in rags, I had been forced to outfit myself in a new uniform to avoid being conscripted into the London County Council Refuse Collection Department.

One straightbacked civilian on Albert Street even reacted aloud, muttering and snorting contemptuously as I strolled by, as if to say, "Bloody twit—staying on in the Army when he could be free to enjoy the promised rewards and benefits of peace."

I didn't mind, especially as he was almost at the end of the unemployment line-up.

I didn't mind. The main thing was I was home. And home was beautiful: a perfect May day in the national capital, the sun shining from a sky clouded only by the smoke from the Eddy Match Company across the river, the sunlight beaming onto tulip and daffodil (one of each in the Capital Commission gardens), and upon the verdigris towers of Parliament. There was hardly a sign of snow, except for a trickling, dirt-speckled heap of the stuff along the wall below the hill.

Though my heart was fluttering about helplessly in its cage of ribs because I felt so breathless with joy and anticipation at seeing my folks again, I forced myself not to hurry, in order to savor the once so familiar sights and sounds, to help convince myself that after four years of combat, politics, death sentences, and other *contretemps,* I really was home again.

There was so much nourishment for the senses, they felt quite bloated. I stared, I sniffed, I tasted, I listened with eye-prickling emotion to the clear, bell-like tones of the North American speech, after one and a half years of the Slavonic rhapsody. "What in tarnation," "Sakes alive," "You ain't kiddin'," "Be seein' ya."

So much was unfamiliar, so much had changed, visibly and invisibly: some new buildings, entirely new fashions, new Prime Ministers—Borden was still P.M., actually, but would be giving up

145

in a few weeks—another blueblood Governor-General had taken over since I first left, in 1916, Laurier had died while I was in the Peter and Paul Fortress in Petrograd. The newspapers were filled with unfamiliar names and references to incomprehensible events —there was talk of a Radio Station to be opened in Pittsburgh. What did that mean? Was it going to broadcast morse code? And there'd been some general strike or other, that had taken place in Winnipeg a year before. And expressions of detestation of the United States, especially now the goldurn Yankees were claiming to have won the war single-handed . . . In spite of which, the country seemed less British and more American. People wore American clothes, drove American cars, whistled American songs—I heard Ted Lewis singing a new hit called *When My Baby Smiles at Me*, on someone's Edison Phonograph—and American business firms were flooding in—possibly to escape something called Prohibition.

The prices had changed, too. The raincoat I had bought for $5 was now $14; a kitchen range, formerly $26 was now, I saw by the shop windows, $40; Chambray dresses were as much as $2, corsets had doubled, cinema prices has soared to 10¢, and you couldn't get a Studebaker for less that $885, or even a Ford for under $530. It was really shocking.

But I wouldn't really have cared even if corsets had risen three times. I was home.

Nearly there now, pale and thin as a poor excuse but joyful as a lark, as I picked my way through the garbage cans in the narrow back street where my parents lived.

A couple of years after my father's *alfresco* cavortings in the barley with a girl called Denise, my parents had come together again, though in somewhat reduced circumstances. In place of the Ontario gingerbread house in Beamington, they now shared a frame house near the Rideau Canal. It was in rather a shabby district, i.e., in the vicinity of Parliament. In fact, it was no more than three minutes' walk from Parliament Hill.

'We finally prevailed on your mother to take him back,' my Aunt Barbara had written—Aunt Barbara was the only forthright relative I had—'And though she says she has neither forgotten nor forgiven, your father doesn't appear to notice much difference in her attitude. But then she was never one to flaunt her feelings, as you know.'

The Reverend Mr. Bandy had, of course, long since lost his stipend. Since being told by the Church to go unfrock himself, he had been eking out a living by writing articles for ecclesiastical journals (under a Latin pseudonym) and adapting his old sermons for sale to other ministers (under a Greek one).

'At the moment,' Aunt Barbara went on, 'they are living in a district in Ottawa where they are least likely to meet any of their former acquaintances. As for how such a man as your father could have come to topple off those high moral principles of his, you will have to work that out for yourself. If you manage to find out, however, please don't tell me, as I now live in Toronto, where we prefer not to hear about animal husbandry and all the other sordid things that go on in the country.'

As a matter of fact, that was one reason I was so anxious to get acquainted with my father, to try to understand how he had come to abandon his belief that words speak louder than actions. I suspected, from my own experience, that he must have had a lot of excess passion locked away behind his dickey and, like the time he tried to drown the deacon's cat in the rainwater barrel, had not had sufficient strength to hold down the lid.

When I first heard about it, my reaction had surprised me. Denise, an exceedingly pretty and quite honest girl, one third my father's age, had figured quite prominently in my own shamefully lascivious dreams. I couldn't understand how father had managed to dandle her on his lapse. She'd never even let *me* see her garters.

I hadn't been so much shocked—as jealous.

And there it was at last.

Home sweet home.

It was hideous. Grass was growing out of the sagging gutter, great flakes of whitish paint curled their lips contemptuously from every clapboard.

Still, in the back garden, glimpsed along a narrow side passage, a glorious magnolia tree exploded out of the backyard clutter, the flagstones strewn with its white, pink-tipped petals.

Heart thudding away like billy-ho, I marched bravely forward— not much of a march, as the front door was only two steps away from the sidewalk—my eyes darting eagerly from window to window, in case mother was looking out for me. I'd telegraphed from

Montreal telling them I was arriving that morning. But the blinds were down against the sun.

I raised a shaky hand to knock. There was a large lady standing in the next doorway. Her hair was all over the place. She looked like a giant sea anemone.

"The meter's round the side," she bellowed. "You lot oughter know that by now."

"I'm not the meter reader. I'm their only begotten son."

"I'm danged. I didn't know they had none," Mrs. Danged said.

"But then, of course," she added, "they never tell me nothin'."

A small child with a bare bum appeared from behind her skirts. I looked away squeamishly, and taking a deep breath, rapped on the door.

"You back bein' a soldier, then? What's the matter, couldn't ya get a job?" When I didn't answer—my throat was too constricted—she muttered, "All right. Stuck-up-back stud. Just like his old man . . . Airs and graces . . . Fuggen wing-collar . . ."

She went in and slammed the door. Locked out, the child started to holler, looking at me in panic.

Mother opened the door.

"Oh, it's you, Bartholomew," she said.

"Mother."

She peered around cautiously. "Were you talking to Mrs. Gore?" she asked. "I wouldn't do that, Bartholomew. It might encourage her."

Safely inside, she embraced me so warmly I felt quite choked up.

"It's wonderful to see you again, Bartholomew."

"Me, too . . ."

The living room was as dark and stifling as the hot room in a Russian *isba*. Father was sitting by a large coal fire in his shirt-sleeves, holding the Bible in a domineering way.

"There's your father," mother said, in case I hadn't noticed him. Then, before the old man could say anything: "When did you get in? I thought you were arriving early this morning?"

"I had to go to the Air Board, Mother."

"That's nice," mother said. "You finding a spare moment to see us."

"Yes, we're very honored, Bartholomew," father said heavily. He was obviously put out because I'd caught him without a collar.

We shook hands. After a warm exchange: "Well, I'll show you your room, Bartholomew," he said. "I expect you'll want to look neat and tidy for dinner."

"Sit down first and have a cup of tea," mother said.

Within a few minutes, I was sweating like a cistern. Even father was plucking a bit moodily at his shirt. Mother's pores, however, remained undemonstrative. Her skin remained as dry as a diploma.

"You don't seem to have gained much weight since you left," she said. "Don't they feed you in the Army?"

"There's a famine in many parts of Russia," I said, and started to tell her about it.

"Why didn't you write?" she asked. "We were worried about you."

"After all, he's a general now, Mother," father said.

"I'm still a lieutenant, really. The rest was just kind of acting temporary."

"I'm glad to see there is still a shade of humility left in you, Bartholomew," said father. "Always remember that in the eyes of God you are less than nothing."

"It's funny," I mused, after a moment. "You remember the last time I was in church, in—" I stopped, not knowing whether to mention Beamington or not. It might be considered a rude word, now. "In your last church? In 1916. You remember, Mother? When I sat between you and Mabel House?"

"I remember you sang very loudly, Bartholomew," mother said with what I was absolutely certain was a fond smile.

"M'yes," I whined. "Anyway, you know what I was thinking about? I was a brand-new sub-lieutenant at the time, and there I was, only just starting out on my military career, already dreaming of becoming a general, and having tea with the Archbishop of Canterbury and everything. Actually, I never met him."

"In that case, Bartholomew," father said, "why are you relating this story?"

"But I did meet the King," I finished, beginning to slump a bit. "The point is, you see, I was also daydreaming about meeting . . . uh . . . him . . . Anyway . . ."

I started to pluck at my wound stripes; but then thought, "Dammit, I'm Major General Bandy, C.B.E., D.S.O. and bar, M.C., D.F.C., et cetera. I sat up straight again.

"That seems rather a pointless sort of story, Bartholomew."

"M'yes," I muttered. "Well, you know what they say in Russia, Papa. *A wet cabbage weighs less than a dry samovar.*"

"Don't be foolish, Bartholomew," Papa said.

Afterward, we sat around the dinner table with what remained of the best silver and linenware, sipping coffee. When I told mother that after that eighteen months in Russia it seemed the best coffee I'd ever had in my life, she leaned over impulsively and tapped me twice on the wrist with her fish fork.

"It's so nice to have you back, Bartholomew," she said tenderly. "I've missed you . . . So much has happened . . ."

"Yes," I said, thinking about those four years.

"You know that Mabel has three children now."

"Ah."

"And your Aunt Beatrice choking on her teeth."

Throughout the meal, father, grown more at ease now that he had his wing-collar on, kept stealing glances at me when he thought I wasn't looking. Despite himself, he was quite plainly filled with wonderment. He was obviously trying to suppress his awe at the remarkable achievements of this son of his, this Knight of the Air and leader of men who had hobnobbed with generals and prime ministers and aroused the ire and admiration of thousands.

I looked back at him, erect and beribboned, sworded and batoned and pipped, authoritative, commanding, ready at the drop of a hint to strip my sleeve and show my scars and say, 'These wounds I had on Crispin's Day,' or words to that effect. I waited agog.

He continued to sit there for the longest time, marvelling at his progeny; this noble, modest, circumspect lad of his who had always been clean-thinking, right-minded, God-fearing, and moved his bowels regularly.

There it was again, that piercing look. Now he was rubbing his temples with thumb and middle finger, one for each temple, and muttering. It sounded like, "Certainly not from *my* side of the family . . ."

"What?" mother asked flatly.

"I just don't understand," he said at length, shaking his head and staring at me openly this time, "where on earth the boy got that face."

I looked around the room, at the chocolate wallpaper and the colorful picture of 'Moses in the Bullrushes,' then down at the early-nineteenth-century library wheelbarrow that my father had used for carting his sermons around the study; and I knew I was home.

PaperJacks

PaperJacks, the newest addition to General Publishing Co. Ltd. (one of the few Canadian book companies owned by Canadians), is the most exciting and innovative Canadian mass market paperback program in Canada. Designed to introduce for the first time in paperback both Canadian books formerly published in hard cover and original works by Canadian authors, PaperJacks includes in its list such noted writers as Robert Thomas Allen, Tom Ardies, Margaret Atwood, Claude Aubry, John B. Ballem, Jack Batten, Clark Blaise, Harry Boyle, Sheila Burnford, Eugène Cloutier, Raymond de Coccola & Paul King, David Conover, Kildare Dobbs, Marian Engel, Alan Fry, Mavis Gallant, Anne Hébert, Piet Hein, Harold Horwood, E. Pauline Johnson, Donald Johnston, Drs. Harold & Oriana Josseau Kalant, Ronald A. Keith, Thomas P. Kelley, Helen Marquis, Fredelle Bruser Maynard, Brian Moore, Audrey Y. Morris, Eric Nicol, Mordecai Richler, R. D. Symons, and Delbert A. Young.

In a short time, PaperJacks has set industry-wide precedents, and will continue to provide good mass market books by important Canadian authors—books needed by Canadians at prices they can afford.